To Catch a
DREAM

ANNE SCHRAFF

SADDLEBACK
EDUCATIONAL PUBLISHING

URBAN UNDERGROUND

SADDLEBACK
EDUCATIONAL PUBLISHING
www.sdlback.com

© 2011 by Saddleback Educational Publishing

ISBN-13: 978-1-61651-269-9
ISBN-10: 1-61651-269-5
eBook: 978-1-60291-994-5

Printed in Guangzhou, China
1010/10-25-10

16 15 14 13 12   1 2 3 4 5

CHAPTER ONE

Y̶ou land a job yet, *muchacho*?" Sal Ruiz asked his son, Abel. Abel Ruiz was a sixteen-year-old junior at Cesar Chavez High School, and he'd been searching for part-time work for more than a month. Every afternoon after classes, he walked around the *barrio* looking for "Help Wanted" signs. Nobody seemed to be hiring.

"Not yet, Dad," Abel answered wearily, dropping his books on the kitchen table and unburdening himself of his backpack. He let the backpack drop to the floor with a thud.

"How come?" his dad asked. Sal Ruiz did hard, backbreaking work for a gardening company owned by his wife's cousin.

He dug planting holes for trees and trimmed shrubs. He carried cement for making patios and built block walls. Nothing was too hard for him to handle. He began working when he was thirteen, and he was almost forty. The work had grown harder, but his body had grown weaker.

"I don't know, Dad," Abel responded. "I've been to lots of places, but they don't need anybody."

"Maybe you're too particular, *muchacho*," Dad suggested.

The family consisted of Abel, his older brother, Tomás, and thirteen-year-old Penelope, whom everybody called "Penny." Liza Ruiz, Abel's mother, didn't work outside the home. But she made beautiful scarves and sold them through high-end boutiques, making good money. But the family had a big mortgage on the house and college expenses for Tomás. They needed all the money everybody could bring in. Tomás was the shining light of the family, having earned straight As at Chavez

High and now studying engineering at UCLA. Abel was clinging to a B minus at Chavez.

"I'd do any kind of work as long as it's legal," Abel told his dad. He was a skinny kid with a bad complexion. He had just one good friend at school, Ernesto Sandoval, who had just moved into town from LA. Ernesto was a great friend, probably the best friend Abel ever had. He was the son of the school's history teacher, Luis Sandoval.

"Have you tried the donut shop?" Liza Ruiz asked, coming into the kitchen with one of her scarves in her hands. "That one on Tremayne is always hiring."

Liza Ruiz was smarter than her husband, and she knew it. She wasn't a cruel person, but she demeaned her husband sometimes. He had dropped out of high school before he graduated, and he'd never had a really good job. He was a jack-of-all-trades and master of none, as the saying went. If Liza's cousin had not given him a job with his landscaping firm, the family would be in dire straits.

"No, I didn't try there," Abel admitted. He glanced at his mother. She was small and trim, younger looking than a mother of three.

Abel believed that his mother thought her smart son, Tomás, took after her, and Abel was more like his father. When Liza was in school, she was an excellent student and very popular with the boys because of her beauty. Tomás was bright and handsome, and he always had plenty of friends too. Like his father, Abel was plain looking and not very smart, and he didn't have many friends. He counted himself really lucky when Ernesto Sandoval became his friend because a lot of kids liked Ernesto.

Once, when Abel's mother was in a very bitter mood, she said to him, "God took pity on me and sent me a son who shines like the stars before sending me my second son." She didn't even know Abel heard that comment. She hadn't meant to hurt him, but he did hear it and it stung. The remark remained in his heart like a scar all these years.

Sal Ruiz did not expect much of Abel either, because he expected little of himself. He only wanted Abel to be willing to work and not to be lazy. Mr. Ruiz did not think Abel would amount to much, just as he had never amounted to much. But if Abel worked hard, as his father did, and was honest, he could make his way in the world. A man could not expect more than that. Mr. Ruiz was at peace with the way the world was set up. When Abel was about ten, he explained his view of life to the boy.

"You see this photograph of a pyramid, *mi hijo*?" he asked. "Do you see how little room there is at the top? This is where the smart and rich are. Now look at the great space at the bottom. That is for the rest of us. There are many more of us than there are of them. But that's all right. We survive."

At times, Abel was not satisfied with the image of the pyramid and what it signified. He wanted more. He was willing to struggle for more. Even at school he studied much harder than most kids. His teachers called him an overachiever.

And now Abel really wanted a job. His friend, Ernesto, worked at the pizzeria, and he saved enough money to buy a car. It was a used car. Worse, it was a horrible Volvo once owned by an old lady, who was now in a nursing home. But at least Ernesto had wheels. Abel wanted a car too, even if it was an old junker. Mom managed the finances in the Ruiz house, and she was very frugal. She insisted that Dad hand over his paycheck every two weeks, and she paid the mortgage and the utilities. She gave Dad a little spending money, just as she gave Abel money for lunches and maybe a pair of socks. No way would she give Abel money for a car.

Ernesto had a beautiful girlfriend, Naomi Martinez, and they'd go driving in the Volvo. Ernesto took Naomi to the movies and to concerts. Abel didn't have a girlfriend, but he hoped to have one eventually. Abel thought that, if he found a girl who was hard up enough to go out with him, he couldn't expect her to ride the bus to the movies with him. He'd have to provide her with a ride. Abel was straining at the bit. He needed money. He needed freedom. He had to get a job.

After school on Tuesday. Abel walked down Tremayne to the donut shop. It was a small place with four tables. Most of its customers bought donuts and other baked goods to go.

When Abel entered the shop, he was struck by the wonderful smells. The display case contained all kinds of donuts, apple fritters, and bear claws. The owner of the place, Elena Suarez, about forty, was a plump, pretty woman who wore too much makeup. She looked like she sampled a lot of her own merchandise.

"Hi, what can I do for you?" she asked Abel, thinking he was a customer.

Abel was so used to going into a place, asking for a job, and then being turned down, that he had little hope here. And his feelings showed. He felt like saying, "I want a job, but you probably don't want to hire me. So I'll just be on my way." He didn't say that, though. He forced himself to smile and speak up. "I'm Abel Ruiz, a junior at Cesar Chavez High School, and I'm looking for a part-time job after school. I got some references from teachers and stuff."

"Yeah?" Elena responded. "Well, go sit at one of the tables and fill out this application. I'll be over to look at it and interview you. I need some help here."

Abel's heart leaped. He had never gotten this far. He never even got an application to fill out. At the hamburger joint and the taco stand, they just said they didn't need anybody.

Abel sat down and began filling out the application. Under "References," he put down the name of Luis Sandoval, his history teacher. He included two other teachers who seemed to like him too. He put down the name of the old lady at the end of the street. A couple times he mowed her lawn. She called him a "nice *muchacho*" when she paid him. Finally, he listed a man on the street who once paid him to help move a piano. After that, the guy always waved to Abel.

Elena Suarez noticed Abel was finished with the application. She came over and sat opposite him at the table. She glanced at the application and commented, "Looks good. Lot of nice references. Well, we need somebody for Monday, Wednesday, and Friday, in the afternoon. I have two employees now, but they can't work some days. I'd need you between four and seven. Would that work for you?"

"Oh yeah," Abel replied, happiness rising in him like a great tide. He couldn't believe he was actually going to get a job. "Yeah, that'd be great, Mrs.—"

"Elena. Everybody calls me Elena," the woman answered. "So, Abel, I'll see you at four tomorrow, okay?"

"You bet. I'll be here," Abel affirmed. He didn't ask about the salary. He just wanted a job. He thought he'd grab the job even if the pay was just a few dollars an hour.

"Oh, it's minimum wage, Abel," Elena went on. "But we got a tip jar, and people are pretty generous. I always split the tips evenly among the kids working on the shift. You might end up with five extra dollars every day you work." She smiled at Abel. Elena had dyed carroty red hair and a bad perm. But at that moment she was the most beautiful creature on earth. She had given Abel a job.

"Thank you, thank you so much," Abel babbled on his way out. The minute he was out of the donut shop, Abel texted his friend Ernesto. "Got the job! Got the job!" Abel didn't have any other friends close enough to care about what was going on in his life. But he'd told Ernesto he was going for the donut shop job. Ernesto had told him about his job at the pizza shop. They were friends.

Abel jogged home. The donut shop was close to where he lived on Sparrow Street. The location was very convenient.

As he burst through the front door of his house, Abel yelled, "They hired me at the donut place!"

"That's great, Abel," Dad responded.

Mom came around the corner and told him, "I thought they'd probably want you. It's easy working at a place like that. Not a lot of complicated orders to get mixed up, like at a hamburger or pizza store. They like to hire kids from school too. It's good for business."

Mom's comment about the orders being uncomplicated—in other words, easier for Abel's slow mind—was not lost on him. He gave her a dirty look.

Penelope was texting her friends from middle school. To Abel, his sister seemed to be texting every waking moment. She looked up and asked, "Will they give you free apple fritters and stuff when you work there?"

Mom glared at her daughter. Penelope wasn't fat, but lately she'd been adding a few too many pounds. "You don't need that greasy garbage, Penny," Mom scolded. "You need broccoli and carrots."

"Ewww!" Penelope cried, without looking up from her phone. She kept on texting her friends.

"Don't you have any homework, Penny?" Mom asked.

"Nope," the girl answered, not even pausing in her texting.

"Penelope Ruiz," Mom growled, "will you stop that? Honestly, I wish they'd never invented those stupid phones."

Penelope rolled her eyes and texted "GTG" to her friend.

The living room of the Ruiz home was nicely furnished. The arrangement was Mom's work. She had good taste. She knew what a few very good pieces could do for a room. She kept within the family budget, making a comfortable and appealing environment. Hanging on the walls were photos of the three Ruiz children. Abel noticed that there were more pictures of Tomás than of anyone else. Tomás graduating from high school as valedictorian. Tomás playing football and making the crucial touchdown for Cesar Chavez High. Tomás as an engineering student at UCLA. Tomás at the prom with a beautiful girl. There were also some photos of Penelope in her soccer uniform and two of Abel. In his freshman photo at Chavez, he looked frightened. The other photo showed him playing basketball before he was dropped from the team.

Despite Mom's favoritism, Abel didn't dislike his older brother. Only two years separated the boys, and they'd been great buddies when they were small. Now, however, Abel was jealous of Tomás. Tomás seemed to have it all, and Abel seemed to have nothing. Perhaps because he was the oldest and first in line when they were passing out good looks, brains, and charm, Tomás seemed to have gotten everything. By the time Abel arrived, nothing was left.

Dad wasn't helpful either. Dad often told Abel that since he was, like his father, not too bright, he'd have to settle for a mediocre life. Dad wasn't trying to be mean. He was just trying to prepare Abel for the real world. Sal Ruiz did not have a mean bone in his body. He reminded Abel of a gentle, amiable mule, working constantly at hard, menial work without complaining, never resting, never getting anywhere. Abel rarely saw the man sitting down. He was either at the job working or doing chores around the house. Abel always saw his father in motion. He expected that one day his father would just drop dead with a shovel or a rake or a mop in his hand. As he breathed his last breath, his Dad would have a patient smile on his face.

Unlike Dad, Mom pointed out Abel's shortcomings in a sharper way. She was clearly disappointed in her younger son. She reminded Abel constantly that, since he had been shortchanged in the intelligence department, he would have to work doubly hard just to stay even.

Tomás also knew that he was the brain in the family, not Abel. He didn't rub that fact in, but he knew it. He made it clear in subtle ways. For instance, he smiled patronizingly when Abel didn't get the drift of something he was talking about. At such times, without meaning to, Abel *did* dislike his brother. He feared he might eventually come to hate him, and he didn't want that to happen.

At dinner that night, Mom announced, "Tomás is coming down for the weekend." She was always happy to see her elder son. "I told him he was probably so busy with all his classes up there at UCLA that maybe he shouldn't take the time to come. But you know Tomás. He wants to see his family."

"Yes," Sal Ruiz agreed. "It will be good to see him." Dad reached for a second helping of *enchiladas*.

"Sal," Mom scolded. "You've already had two *enchiladas*, and a big pile of refried beans."

Dad held his fork in midair, looking forlornly at the third *enchilada* his mouth waited for. Like Penelope, he wasn't fat. But he was getting a big belly, and that angered his wife. She was always reading medical reports on the risks of obesity.

"You know what the doctors say about fat around the midsection, Sal," Mom reminded him.

Dad put down his fork in defeat.

"Sal, you haven't even touched your salad." Mom spoke to her husband in the same tone of voice she used for her children. The only time Mom used a tone of respect to a member of the family was when she was speaking to Tomás.

Abel felt sorry for his father. Without meaning to be unkind, Mom demeaned him all the time. Anything she said was always for his own good, but Abel wondered whether she didn't make his father feel like less of a man.

"The salad is gross," Penelope remarked, wrinkling her nose.

"No, it's not," Mom snapped. "It's delicious. You would be better off, Penny, if you ate more salads and fruits. Do you want to get to look like Aunt Marla?"

Dad's sister, Marla, was quite heavy. Abel thought she looked fine because she was square and solid. She didn't bulge out in places as many heavy women did. She was a nice person too. Aunt Marla was one of Abel's favorite relatives, if not the most favorite. She was always very kind to Abel, giving him compliments and nice gifts, usually money.

"I don't look like Aunt Marla," Penelope shrieked.

"Don't scream at the table, young lady," Mom commanded. "Next year you'll be a freshman at Chavez High. Don't you want to be nice and slim like the pretty girls? As we all know, Aunt Marla never married, and that surely was because of her weight problem."

Having been denied his third *enchilada*, Dad was a rare bad mood. He was never cross, but sometimes, infrequently, he dared to disagree with Mom. "My sister, Marla, she never wanted to get married" Dad objected. "Even when we were children, she told me she didn't want to get married. She's an RN now, the head one in surgery. She's very happy and fulfilled. She earns good money, and she takes trips all over the world. She went to Spain with her friends last year and she had a wonderful time."

"Yes," Mom sighed, unwilling to be contradicted, "she puts on a brave front. And tells everybody she never wanted to be married, but I'm not so sure. I've always felt sorry for spinsters." Mom refused to give up her view of Marla Ruiz as a miserable, lonely woman who never had boyfriends because she was a size sixteen, instead of a size six, like Mom.

Abel thought about his job at the donut shop, and he felt happy. He'd be earning some money, and he could pick up a used car of his own. He already had a driver's license. He'd gotten it on his first try down at the DMV, to the shock of his mother. The thought of driving around on his own thrilled him.

Sometimes being in the Ruiz household frustrated Abel so much that he wanted to beat his fists on the wall. Penelope annoyed him, and Mom was on his case around the clock. Dad—poor Dad—sat there like a beaten-down beast of burden. And the sight of him like that depressed Abel because it seemed like a preview of his own future.

Tomás, when he was around, was the worst. Everyone considered Tomás handsome. He had such big white teeth that, when he smiled, he seemed to light up the room. But Abel thought Tomás looked a little bit like a horse when he smiled.

CHAPTER TWO

When Abel reported to work at Elena's Donut Shop the next afternoon, Wednesday, he was nervous. He didn't bring much experience to the job. But he had helped his mother dole out donuts at Our Lady of Guadalupe Church after the 7:30 mass on Sundays. Sometimes he dished out the donuts, and sometimes he took in the dollar and a quarter for coffee and a donut. Abel could make change pretty well; so he thought that wouldn't be a problem. Still, this was his first real job.

When Abel arrived, Elena introduced him to the other two employees on that shift. Claudia Villa was a sweet-looking girl who wore big, round glasses. "Hi Abel," she greeted him in a friendly voice. Her golden brown eyes sparkled behind the glasses.

Paul Morales was eighteen. He had already graduated from Chavez High, and he was taking classes in a technical school. He looked at Abel and advised, "Some guy always comes in around this time, a fat guy. He always wants three dozen assorted donuts. He takes forever to pick them out. Kinda hurry him along if other customers are in line."

Abel stood alongside Paul for the first hour. He was really fast. He whipped out the orders and kept the line moving. "People hate to stand in line," Paul told Abel. "Get 'em in and out," Paul said. He seemed like a smart guy. He reminded Abel of Tomás.

Paul worked until six and then left for home. Between six and seven, Claudia and Abel worked. (Elena Suarez then usually kept the shop open until around eight. A few customers came in the evening to buy half-priced donuts for the next morning.)

Right after Paul left, Abel was at the counter when the big man came in for his three dozen donuts. He grinned at Abel and asked, "You're new, huh? I come here every day. I bring donuts in for the guys at the factory where I work. Ah, let's see now, what do I want?"

A slender, impatient-looking woman was already in line behind the big man. She was shifting her weight from one foot to the other.

"How about a dozen chocolate and a dozen glazed?" Abel suggested. "And the rest assorted."

"Ahhh, those nutty ones look awfully good," the big man commented. "Let's have a half dozen of those. Let me see . . ."

The woman behind him was sighing. All she wanted was a donut and coffee.

"I can help you here," Claudia said to her, coming in after a break. The woman rushed over to make her purchase and she rushed out, her high heels clicking on the floor.

"Umm, like maybe four of those jelly ones," the man went on, "and the ones with sprinkles on the top, half dozen of those." He was peering into the display case. "How many I got now?"

Abel's head was spinning. He hadn't been keeping track. "Um, let's see," Abel counted. "You got sixteen so far."

A line was forming again. Two rough-looking workmen waited behind a pair of teenagers in baggy clothing with tattoos on their hands. One of the boys had a shaved head and a tat of a dragon on the back of his hand.

"Let's put one of each kind in here," Abel suggested, "and then we got three dozen."

"Hey, not so fast!" the big man complained. "The boys down at the factory don't like those filled ones."

"Hey man," complained the boy with the dragon tattoo. "Hurry it up. We ain't got all night."

The big man turned and looked indignantly at the boy. "I'm sure you have very important things to do," he responded in a snide voice. "Like maybe tag some fences or maybe rob a liquor store."

Abel felt cold and dizzy.

"I can help you guys over here," Claudia sang out with her warm smile. As she gave the teenagers their change, one of them snarled, "*Puerco*! Maybe he shouldn't eat three boxes of donuts!"

The big man turned, seeming to spoil for a fight. But the boys were already going out the door.

"Dirty little punks," he fumed. "Gang-bangers. Lousy little criminals. You think they ever went to work in their stinking lives? Probably got a mom who's a welfare queen, milkin' the system and living off working guys like me." He paid for his three dozen donuts and stomped out of the store.

Abel turned to Claudia. "Boy Claudia, you were good," he complimented her. "I was afraid there'd be a fight in here."

"That big man," Claudia explained. "He's very rude. He doesn't care how many people he keeps waiting. He's going to take his sweet time. But he's a customer, and we have to be nice to the customers."

Abel couldn't remember seeing Claudia at Cesar Chavez High School. She looked to be about sixteen. If she was, then she was a junior like Abel. But he never saw her in any of his classes or even on campus. "You go to school at Chavez?" he asked her.

"No, I'm a junior at a private school. Catholic," she replied.

"Isn't that real expensive?" Abel asked.

"Yeah," Claudia admitted, "but they let me do stuff around the school to help with the tuition. And then I work so I can help my parents with the cost. I'm an only child, and my parents put all their hopes and dreams on me. They want to protect me, I guess. You go to Chavez, Abel?"

"Yeah," Abel answered. "I live around here, on Sparrow. I can walk to school and here."

"Is Chavez a good school?" Claudia asked.

"Yeah, it's okay. We got some good teachers. I got this real good friend there, Ernie. His dad teaches history, and he's great. I like his class a lot. But I'm not a real great student," Abel said with a dry laugh. "I guess I'm not real great at anything."

"Oh, don't say that," Claudia objected. Her big, beautiful brown eyes kept getting Abel's attention. She had a lovely little heart-shaped face and clear light mocha skin. "I bet you're good at a lot of things. I can tell right off that you're a nice guy, and that's worth a lot. I can spot a phony a mile off, and you're the real thing."

Her compliment touched Abel. He didn't get many of them. "Thanks," he said. Abel never had a girlfriend in high school. Today, for the first time, he met a girl he thought maybe could be a friend. Abel thought it would be nice to know a girl he felt comfortable with and go for a pizza with . . . or something like that.

Abel and Claudia worked well together. She was friendly, courteous, and efficient.

She taught Abel a lot of little things that Paul skipped over,. She told him to be sure he asked customers how many creams they wanted for their coffee and always to refill the cream thermos on the counter.

Elena showed up at seven. "Well, Abel, how did your first shift go?" she inquired.

"It was good," Abel reported. "I liked it."

"He was very good, Elena," Claudia piped up. "That big guy who's always wanting three dozen donuts came in. Then we got a little busy, but Abel kept cool and got everybody taken care of. Coupla kids with shaved heads and tats came in and gave the big man a hard time, but Abel kept the lid on everything."

"Well, good," Elena said, smiling at Abel. "I had a good feeling about you. I knew right away you'd do well."

Elena checked the tip jar. Eight dollars were already in there. "When you come in on Friday, Abel, I'll give you your share. Probably be more than five dollars."

When Elena went into the back room, Abel looked at Claudia with a questioning look. She'd made Abel sound good, much better than he was. Claudia, not Abel, had kept things moving and cool. Abel was touched by what a nice girl she was. Maybe, he thought, she sort of liked him. He found that notion hard to believe, but maybe it was so. She was a pretty girl but not strikingly beautiful like Naomi Martinez. Naomi turned heads wherever she went. But maybe Claudia didn't have that many guys interested in her. Maybe, Abel thought, he had a chance with her.

Or maybe Claudia was just being nice because Abel was new. Maybe she wanted to give the new guy a leg up. Maybe she meant to do no more than that.

With his share of the tips, Abel figured he earned about twenty dollars today. In five working days, he could have a hundred. Abel's heart raced at the idea. A hundred dollars didn't add up to a fortune by any means, but it did add up. Aunt Marla

usually gave Abel fifty dollars for his birthday and for Christmas. He'd been saving
that. Other relatives gave him socks, but
Aunt Marla gave him nice, crisp bills. Abel
had about six hundred saved from his
aunt's gifts.

Abel sometimes had a fantasy about
going to Aunt Marla's cozy little condo on
Cardinal Street and begging her to let him
move in with her. Then he wouldn't get so
depressed listening to Mom putting Dad
down and Dad taking it like a poor mule. At
Aunt Marla's, he wouldn't have to hear
Mom comparing Abel to Tomás and
wondering why Abel couldn't be more like
his brother. He wouldn't have to put up
with one of Penelope's tantrums over a zit
on her nose.

Cardinal Street was the nicest street
in the *barrio*. It was at the very end
of Tremayne. On that street, all the old
single-family homes that had outlived
their usefulness had been torn down and
replaced by stylish condos with a Spanish

architecture motif. The condos even had pools. On hot summer days, Abel imagined himself going swimming.

When Abel got home after work, Mom was finishing another beautiful scarf that would sell at the boutique for more than Dad made in three days.

"How was your job, Abel?" Mom asked. "Did everything go all right?" She was frowning, and worry underscored her eyes. She clearly expected that Abel had had problems of some form or another on his first day. Abel suspected that she was just hoping and praying the problems were not too serious. She feared he may have already been fired. She loved Abel dearly, just as she loved Tomás and Penelope. In fact, deep in her heart, she loved Abel more because she thought he was so weak and inept. She worried about his making his way in the world.

"Everything went great, Mom!" Abel declared. "I like working there, and the people are nice. Elena, the boss, she's real good. This guy Paul broke me in, and this girl

Claudia, she's really sweet. They showed me all the little things I needed to know, and it was fun dealing with the customers. It was sorta like serving donuts to the people after mass, Mom. Everybody was nice and friendly." Abel had a big smile on his face, and usually he didn't.

Mom was surprised, even disconcerted, by Abel's enthusiasm. She was used to Abel looking glum. "Well, that's wonderful," she responded. Then her worries took over. "You're telling me the truth, aren't you, Abel? I mean, I hope you're not making this all up just to make me feel good. They didn't actually let you go in the first hour or something?"

Mom caught herself and explained her reaction to Abel. "When your dad and I were first married, before I got my cousin to hire him, he'd lie about how he was doing at his various jobs. He just didn't want to worry me. I mean, it's hard to believe things went that well on your very first shift at the donut shop."

"It's true, Mom. Everything was great," Abel asserted, feeling very angry.

"Abel," his mother persisted, "do you remember that time our church asked people to deliver the Thanksgiving baskets to the poor families? You got all mixed up. You delivered the small turkeys to the huge families and the big twenty-pound turkeys to the old couples who had tiny ovens. I've come to expect things don't always go well for you . . ."

"Mom, I was ten years old," Abel protested with disgust. Mom had a way of deflating his best moods. He figured if he ever won a million dollars in the lottery when he was old enough to play, Mom would find a way to ruin the moment. "Honest, Mom, I had a good day at the donut shop, and everything is fine. It's all good." He headed for his room, deeply angry. He feared he would say something to his mother that he would later regret.

Penelope stopped Abel in the hallway before he got to his room. "Did you bring me a chocolate donut like you promised you would, Abel?" she demanded. She stood there, her hands on her hips, looking belligerent. "Yes," Abel thought but didn't say, "she *is* getting fat!"

"I bet you forgot!" she accused him. "You *always* forget! You're just like Daddy!"

"Penny, I didn't forget," Abel told her. "I just didn't do it, and I never promised you I would. A donut would've cost me a dollar. I didn't feel like spending a dollar to bring you home a donut that you don't need. You've been eating chocolate bars in your room. I saw the wrappers on the floor."

"Don't snitch on me!" Penelope warned. "Anyways, I thought they gave you donuts free when you work there."

"No, I woulda had to spend a dollar," Abel said.

"Well, don't ask me for any favors, Abel," Penelope snapped. "If you can't even buy me a lousy chocolate donut, don't expect any favors from me."

"When did you ever do me any favors?" Abel asked his sister as he was finally able to escape to his room.

Abel knew you were supposed to love your family, and he did. He loved his parents because they were good people, and they loved him and took care of him. He loved his brother and sister too. What was love anyway? Wasn't it just wishing well for people and wanting them to be happy? Abel wanted all the people in his family to be as happy as they could be.

But Abel didn't *like* any of them very much. Liking people, to Abel, meant wanting to spend time with them, and Abel didn't enjoy the time he spent with his family. Dad was always depressing Abel with his pyramid stories. He was always dooming Abel to a life at the bottom of the pyramid with all the other miserable losers. No matter how much Abel struggled and clawed, he'd never get to the pinnacle of the pyramid. Mom was absolutely sure of Abel's incompetence at whatever he tried. Penelope was a self-centered little brat. And Tomás . . . well, Tomás looked down on Abel. Tomás regarded Abel not in a mean way, but as arrogant and kindly rich people look down on the poor as they toss them coins. "Here, poor fool," Abel could picture his brother saying, "I know you'll waste this precious quarter I'm giving you, but go for it."

When Abel went to school on Friday, he was actually looking forward to the afternoon and going to work at the donut shop. Working with Claudia was a big plus. But just being there with her would be fun.

At lunch with Ernesto and Ernie's friend from the track team, Julio Avila, Abel talked about his new job. "I really like my job," Abel announced. "It's the best thing that happened to me in a long time."

"Great!" Ernesto said. "That's how I felt when I got the job in the pizzeria. It's kinda fun, and the money sure comes in handy. They like you, huh Abel? I knew they would. You're low-key, but the friendliness in you really comes through. I bet you're great with the customers."

Abel looked at his friend gratefully. Those words meant so much to him: "They like you, huh Abel? *I knew they would*." That's how Ernesto was. He could make you feel like a million dollars when you started out feeling like two cents. Abel had no close friend until Ernesto came on campus a few months ago. The boys hit it off together at once. Now Abel had the feeling there was nothing Ernesto wouldn't do for him, and he felt the same toward Ernesto.

"There's a girl down there, Claudia Villa," Abel continued. "She's extra nice. She's got these big beautiful brown eyes. She wears these big round glasses, and she's so cute . . ."

"Uh-oh!" Julio Avila exclaimed.

Abel looked at Julio. "Uh-oh what?" he asked.

Julio laughed and spoke to Ernesto. "Our *amigo* is falling for a chick," he chuckled. "All the signs are there."

"Nah, nothing like that," Abel protested, laughing too. "But she's so nice and friendly. And she really talked me up to the boss, made me look good. She praised me more than I deserved."

"She go to Chavez?" Ernesto asked.

"No, she goes to a private school," Abel replied. "She said she's an only child and her parents want to protect her by sending her to this private school. She said they're making a lot of sacrifices to afford the tuition. It costs a lot, and Claudia works at the donut shop to help pay for it."

Ernesto clapped Abel on the back. "I'm happy for you man. Nothing like nailing down that first job. It's like welcome to the working world. Before that you're a kid, and now we're wage slaves. Hooray!"

After the last bell that day, Abel hurried over to Elena's Donut Shop a little earlier than he had to. He didn't want to risk being late. But when he walked in, he was struck by the strange atmosphere. The place wasn't as cheerful and happy as it was on Wednesday.

Elena Suarez looked stressed, like she was having a problem. Neither Paul Morales nor Claudia Villa had arrived yet. They weren't due until four, about ten minutes away.

Elena's face was red. She was madly going through the cash drawer, counting and recounting. She looked up at Abel and said, "There's a problem. Some money is missing. I'm missing a hundred dollars from Wednesday's receipts."

Abel felt like somebody had just dumped a bucket of ice water on his head. He stood there, stunned.

Did she think he took the money?

CHAPTER THREE

Perhaps Elena Suarez saw the look on Abel's face. "I may have miscounted or something," she added. "I don't know where my mind is. Oh Abel, what a way to greet you!"

She smiled nervously and explained herself. "I'm really stressed lately. I'm a single Mom, you know. I guess you *don't* know. Anyway, I just went through a nasty divorce, and I have a thirteen-year-old girl who's going through her own teenaged angst. Oh dear. I'm sorry, Abel. Excuse me. I shouldn't be dumping on you."

"I'm sorry," Abel mumbled. He didn't know what else to say. He wished with all his heart that the others would show up. He wanted to see Claudia and Paul, especially Claudia.

Claudia appeared first. "I'm not late, am I?" she asked. "My phone says it's not four yet."

"No, you're fine, Claudia," Elena assured her. "I was just telling Abel. I'm missing a hundred dollars from Wednesday's receipts, but maybe I miscounted. I don't know sometimes if I'm on foot or on horseback."

Paul Morales arrived a few minutes later. He spent his first ten minutes at the shop filling the display cases with fresh pastries from the back. He kept glancing at Elena Suarez, a strange look on his face. When Elena put on her coat and rushed out, Paul remarked, "There's a nutcase if I've ever seen one."

"Oh Paul," Claudia objected. "She's just going through a bad patch in her life. The divorce was really bad, and her exhusband just disappeared on them. The little girl is messed up, and, well, Elena has a right to be a little nuts."

"No wonder her husband didn't hang around," Paul responded. "She probably made a mess of the family finances like she's screwing up around here. She has no business sense. We needed to bake more bear claws. People always asking for them. Instead she bakes six dozen sprinkles that nobody wants, except the fat guy. Then she puts two boxes of jelly donuts in the back behind some junk. She doesn't even get them in the display case. Now they're hard as rocks. I had to throw them out."

Paul shook his head. He again reminded Abel of his brother, Tomás. Tomás had very little patience with stupid people.

"I feel kind of sorry for her," Claudia countered. "She's dealing with a lot."

"You woulda felt sorry for the captain on the *Titanic*, Claudia," Paul told her. "But would you want to go down with the ship? I'm afraid we're gonna get tangled up in this mess, you guys. She's gonna get her money in a big mess. Then she's gonna start thinking one of us is helping themselves to her receipts. Then we got major trouble."

Abel was terrified. He couldn't imagine how he'd feel if Elena accused him of stealing her money. Nobody in the Ruiz family had ever run afoul of the law. Abel had seen the police come to many houses in the *barrio* and take people away, handcuffed. Parents would be standing in the driveway weeping or staring in sorrow. The very thought of bringing that sort of disgrace to his family made Abel sick. Cold chills went through his soul. It was bad enough that Mom thought he was a loser, but if he was ever tainted by a crime!

Maybe, Abel thought hopefully, Paul was exaggerating. Elena Suarez seemed like such a nice lady. Surely she wouldn't accuse some poor kid of robbing her just because she couldn't keep her own books straight.

"Hey Paul," Abel said, "I don't think Elena would ever think we took her money. She's not that kind of a person. Besides, we're honest."

Paul laughed and spoke sharply. "What kind of a fairyland do you come from, Abel? You're too trusting. People, especially old people, don't think much of kids. They think we're all crooks."

"Elena isn't old," Abel objected.

"She's old enough man," Paul affirmed. "She's the same age as my grandmother, and my grandmother thinks anybody under thirty-five is a gangbanger. Elena probably feels the same way. She's been married a coupla times. She had this kid when she was in her forties. She's got a few face-lifts, and she looks pretty young. But she's *old*."

Paul looked Abel right in the eye, "Trust me man, we could be heading for real trouble. I wouldn't be surprised if the lady was buzzed half the time or on pills. Women like her, they take pills to sleep, pills to wake up. They don't buy their junk from some dealer on the street. No, some so-called doctor in a nice office gives them what they want. Look at what's been happening to all these celebs. One day they're smiling on TV, and the next day they're in the morgue. They never met a street pusher. They got it all written on legal pads in the doctor's office."

Paul went into the back of the shop soon after the conversation. He had to set up all the ingredients for Elena in the morning. There was a list of things he had to do. Elena relied on him to have everything ready for her in the morning. She came in at three to do the baking.

Abel and Claudia took over the counter. They were very busy for about an hour. Just as things slowed down, four middle schoolers came in. The girls were only thirteen, but they looked much older. They wore short skirts and tops that didn't cover much in the middle. One of them, a dark-eyed girl with blonde streaks in her chestnut brown hair, was extremely pretty. She came over to the counter and looked right at Abel. "You're new," she declared. "I've never seen you before. Who're you?"

"I'm Abel Ruiz. I just started working here," Abel told the girl. "What would you like? The donuts are fresh, and the apple fritters are real good too."

The girl fixed her gaze on Abel. "You go to Chavez?" she asked.

"Yeah, I'm a junior there," he replied.

"I'm gonna be a freshman there next year if I'm still around this dump of a neighborhood," she remarked. "I'm so done with middle school. I'm so over that creepy place. You're kinda cute, Abel Ruiz. You got a girlfriend?"

Abel was shocked. The girl was thirteen years old, and she acted like a senior in high school or something. She giggled and spoke to her friends. "Look at how his eyes are popping outta his head. Hey Abel Ruiz, didn't you ever see a girl with a pierced belly button before?"

"Come on, Sarah," Claudia chided. "Just order something and go sit down. Like Abel said, the apple fritters are fresh and really good."

"Old four-eyes there probably has her eye on Abel Ruiz too," Sarah commented scornfully. "But you're not hot enough girl. Deal with it." Sarah leaned on the counter then and looked right at Abel. "So, cute guy, you got a girlfriend or not?"

"Stop fooling around, Sarah," Claudia advised. "Leave Abel alone. I'm gonna tell your mom. You're a thirteen-year-old kid, and you're acting like some bad girl. You behave yourself, Sarah, or I'm gonna tell your mom."

"Oooooo, I'm scared!" Sarah cried with mock terror. Her companions laughed. "Okay, we'll have two apple fritters, and we'll split 'em."

Abel put two large apple fritters on the tray, and Sarah and the three others walked to a table and sat down. They all immediately started texting, and Sarah took some pictures of Abel on her cell phone.

"Wow," Abel commented to Claudia, "she doesn't seem like a little thirteen-year-old. I got a sister that age, and she's no way like that."

"She's freaky," Claudia responded. "That's Elena Suarez's daughter."

"You're kidding me," Abel gasped. "*That's* her daughter? No wonder the poor lady's wigged out. Having that kid around would be enough to drive anybody crazy."

Two juniors from Chavez then came in for donuts. Abel recognized Dom Reynosa. He was one of the guys who recently painted a beautiful mural on the side of the science building at Chavez High. He and his friend, Carlos Negrete, were taggers getting ready to drop out. Then Ernesto's father got them interested in the mural and gave them a reason to stay in school. Now it looked as though both would go on to be seniors and graduate.

"Hey Dom," Sarah sang out, "I saw the cool mural you and Carlos did at Chavez. Come on over and sit with us. It's boring to just have girls at a table."

Dom looked at Carlos, and both boys laughed. Carlos ordered two mochas, and then he turned to Sarah. "Hey *niña*, I got a little brother about your age. He likes to ride skateboards. Maybe you and him can be friends."

Abel felt sorry for Elena Suarez. Now that he saw Sarah, he could understand why she was losing money and mixing up orders. Abel's sister, Penelope, seemed like an angel compared to this girl. Maybe today, Abel thought, he would bring Penelope home a chocolate donut, a small one.

Every time a teenaged boy, most of them over sixteen, came into the donut shop, Sarah flirted with them. Then a pair of boys with shaved heads and tattoos came in. Sarah yelled, "Like your tats, boys. They're cool."

"Okay," Claudia muttered to herself. She strode over to the table where Sarah and her companions sat. "You guys've been here long enough. Hit the road. I'm not kidding, Sarah. If you're not gone from here in two minutes, I'm calling your mom on her cell."

"Okay, wicked witch of the west," Sarah complained, getting up. "But Abel

Ruiz likes *me*. I can tell. You haven't got a chance with him." With that, Sarah and her friends left.

One of the boys with shaved heads laughed and asked, "She *loca*?"

Abel and Claudia continued working the rest of their shift. As they did, Abel thought about how he wanted to talk with someone about what was going on at the shop. Right now he was worried sick about the missing money at the donut shop. He kept hearing Paul's dire predictions of serious trouble ahead for them. What if Elena was really irresponsible? What if she kept losing money and started accusing the staff? That could be awful. Abel wished he could just quit this job and get another one. But he liked the job, and he especially liked working with Claudia. And he didn't think he'd get another job anytime soon.

Ernesto Sandoval was always telling Abel how he talked over his problems with his parents, usually his father. Whenever something was bothering Ernesto, he was always so relieved to have a sympathetic ear that he trusted. Ernesto said he didn't always take his father's advice. But listening to someone he loved and trusted helped him make up his mind.

Abel didn't have someone to go to like that. He wanted to talk to somebody about what was going on, but he couldn't talk to his father. Dad was weak. He'd get all upset and tell Mom. Dad would be certain that Abel was about to be embroiled in a dangerous situation, maybe accused of theft. After all, that sort of thing happened to the losers on the bottom. The ones at the top got away with murder, but Abel could easily get blamed and be arrested. Mom would be indignant if she learned what was happening. She would demand that Abel quit the job immediately. Abel could hear her angry voice in his head.

"Abel, I want you out of there immediately," she would command him. "This crazy lady could get you in trouble, and your whole life would be ruined. Abel, it's not worth it. God knows I've had enough trouble already. I don't need police officers knocking on my door and taking my son away."

So talking with either of his parents was out of the question for Abel. Even Tomás would laugh with his big horse teeth and say, "Leave it to you, *chico*. You're in another mess!"

After work, Abel jogged down to Wren Street, where Ernesto Sandoval lived. When Abel hit the doorbell, Maria Sandoval, Ernesto's mother, answered. "Hi Abel," she greeted him with her usual warm smile. "Come on in."

"Hi, Mrs. Sandoval," Abel responded. He also greeted Mr. Sandoval, who was sitting in the living room. "Ernie home?" he asked them.

"Sure," Ernesto's mom answered. "He's downloading some music." She nodded toward Ernesto's room.

"Hi Abel," eight-year-old Katalina yelled. She was putting together a jigsaw puzzle with her grandmother.

"Hello Abel," six-year-old Juanita called out. "You want a piece of cheesecake? Mom just made cheesecake."

Katalina tossed her head in her usual bossy way. "Juanita, Abel works at a bakery. Don't you think he's sick of sweets?"

Abel smiled at the family. Whenever he visited Ernesto's house, he wished he lived here. He wished he were Ernie's brother. But at least he was his best friend.

Abel stood at the door to Ernesto's room. "Hey Ernie," he said.

"Hey Abel. Come on in," Ernesto invited him. "I'm downloading some salsa music. It's pretty good. It's from Oscar Perez. I'm tellin' you man, that dude may be from our *barrio*, but he's going places. He's gonna be the hottest thing outta this place. What's up, Abel? You look worried."

"Well, you know, Ernie," Abel started to say as he sat on the edge of the bed. "I love my job down at the donut shop, and everything was going great. But Elena, the boss, she hit us with a big one today. She's missing a hundred bucks from the receipts. She didn't accuse anybody. Like she even admitted she maybe made a mistake in counting. She said she's got a lot of family stress and stuff. But this dude who works there, Paul Morales, he thinks she's gonna keep on losing money. Sooner or later she's gonna accuse the employees of stealing from her, and we'll be in a lot of trouble. It's got me really worried, Ernie." Abel was so eager to unburden himself that he got the whole story out without taking a breath.

"Mmm," Ernesto mused, "you work alone at the register, Abel?"

"Sometimes. Usually Claudia and me or Paul and me work together," Abel replied.

"Claudia, she's the chick you like, huh?" Ernesto asked.

"Yeah, she's great," Abel grinned. "She thinks Elena is just confused and she'd never actually accuse anybody. Claudia thinks she trusts us, but Paul laughs that off. He's kinda cynical."

"Abel, you mind if we bring my dad in on this?" Ernesto asked.

"No, Ernie, that'd be fine," Abel agreed. Abel liked and trusted Luis Sandoval, not only as his teacher but as a person anybody could go to with a problem.

Ernesto went called out to his dad in the living, and his father came to the room. Luis Sandoval listened to Abel's story. "Well, Abel," Mr. Sandoval responded, "I'm glad you mentioned this to us. You've given your friends a heads-up in case something does happen. You've probably got nothing to be concerned about. But if this Elena does make an accusation, we know what's happening and we could help."

That answer alone made Abel feel better. "In the meantime," Mr. Sandoval continued, "you've got to be very careful not to make any mistakes with the cash. And your crew needs to have each other's backs. Always make sure two people count the money. Be alert to what's going on. Look out for each other. I don't think you should quit the job as long as you like it and you're doing well. It doesn't look good on a guy's résumé if he quits jobs real soon after getting them."

Abel smiled at Ernesto and his father. "Thanks, you guys. I feel a lot better. I just had to tell somebody. And, you know, everything at my house gets to be a big deal and . . ."

"How is your family, Abel?" Mr. Sandoval asked. "Your dad doing okay? I met him at the gas station the other day, and he said he's got a bad backache."

"Yeah, he's working hard," Abel replied. "He's a landscaper you know, and he's always lifting heavy stuff. He does some brick walls and, you know, puts in little waterfalls. He likes that part of the job. He calls what he usually does stoop labor."

"I was over on Cardinal Street the other day," Mr. Sandoval commented. "And I saw your dad working at a condo. He was making this really beautiful wall and a little koi pool. It looked really great. He was arranging the brickwork, and it was impressive. You could tell he really knew what he was doing."

Mr. Sandoval cocked his head a little, lost in thought for a moment. Then he spoke again. "I bet if you guys walked around the neighborhood you'd find a lot of beautiful spots he created. He has an artistic flair, that's for sure. The *barrio* surely isn't an upscale place, but it ought to give your dad a lot of satisfaction to know how much beauty he has created around here."

"Thanks," Abel said. "I'm gonna tell my dad that. He'll like to hear that. He doesn't get too many compliments. He doesn't think much of himself or what he does."

"Well, you tell him that he's making a lasting impact around here. That's a lot more than many people can say," Ernesto's father replied.

When Abel and Ernesto were alone again, Abel said, "That was so cool of your dad to say that stuff about my dad's work.

I think when Dad was a young guy, he wanted to start his own business building walls and fountains and stuff, but that never happened. Now he just works without thinking too much about anything except the end of the day and coming home to dinner."

Abel sat quietly for a moment, feeling sorry for his father. Mom loved Dad, Abel thought. But as time went by, she thought more and more of him as a nice, kindly dolt who never did accomplish anything of value.

Ernesto probably read his friend's mind. "Abel," he said suddenly, "you want to go to the auto show on Saturday? You texted me that you'd like to go, and I got tickets."

"Yeah, that'd be great," Abel agreed. "I can pay for my ticket now that I'm working."

"No, that's okay," Ernesto insisted. "I got two tickets. I was thinking Naomi would want to go with me. But she said an auto show is about as interesting as watching a column of ants go down the sidewalk. She thinks it's the most boring thing in the world. If she went, she'd just be doing it for me. She'd be miserable. So I'd be glad if you went with me, Abel."

"Okay!" Abel said happily.

"I'll pick you up around ten, and we'll have a blast looking at all the great cars we can't afford until we're too old to enjoy them!" Ernesto laughed.

Abel left the Sandoval house feeling much better than he did when he arrived. He had bought a chocolate donut for his little sister because meeting Sarah Suarez had made him see Penelope's virtues. He also had a big compliment for his father to deliver from Luis Sandoval. It would mean a lot to a man who got little praise from anybody.

CHAPTER FOUR

Abel was walking home briskly in the dark when he saw her. "Hey Abel Ruiz," Sarah sang out. "Now that the wicked witch of the west is gone, let's do something!"

"*Are you crazy, Sarah?*" Abel yelled at the girl. "Girl, go home! It's dark."

Sarah came closer, almost touching him. "You liked me when you saw me in the donut shop. I could tell. You kept staring at me like I really turned you on."

"Sarah," Abel protested, taking a step back, "I'm a junior in high school. I'm sixteen years old. You're a little girl. You're in middle school. What are you doing on the street at this hour? Where's your mom?"

"I've dated lots of boys who're sixteen," Sarah declared. "It's no big deal."

"You're lying, Sarah," Abel accused her. "You gotta go home to your mother. What's the matter with you?"

"Mom's not home," Sarah told him. "She's never home. I hang out at the twenty-four-seven store. I got a lotta friends there."

"I bet your mom's at the donut shop," Abel responded. "You better go over there. It's dangerous for a little girl to be by herself at night around here."

"Stop calling me a little girl," Sarah commanded. "I'm not a little girl. I'm taller than my mother. And I'm not scared of the street. I'm not scared of anything."

"There are gangbangers out here when it gets dark," Abel warned. He was getting a headache. He was scared. He didn't know what to do. Finally he pulled out his cell phone and told her, "I'm calling your mom on her cell and telling her to come get you, Sarah."

"Don't you dare rat me out, Abel Ruiz," Sarah ordered, her eyes on fire. "Anyway, Mom doesn't care. She doesn't even know I exist. Daddy was different. Me and Daddy were close, but she made his life miserable. Now he's in Rosarito Beach at Uncle Hilario's crab shack. He's lucky. He doesn't have to be around Mom anymore."

No way Abel was going to get mixed up with this *niña loca*.

Abel looked desperately around the street. Even though it was dark, a lot of boys were still skateboarding. They looked like middle schoolers, twelve or thirteen years old. Abel recognized Carlos Negrete's little brother, Estebán. He was a tough little eleven-year-old. When a speeding car almost hit him on the street, he tracked down the car to the parking lot at Cesar Chavez High School and keyed it. That wasn't the right thing to do, but, no doubt about it, Estebán was tough.

"Hey Estebán!" Abel called out.

Estebán picked up his skateboard and came toward Abel. "Hey man, what's goin' down?" the boy asked.

"Estebán, you know Sarah here?" Abel asked.

Estebán made a sour face. "Yeah," he said.

"Will you take Sarah to the donut shop where her mom is? I'm worried about a little girl being out here at night. Will you do that for me, Estebán?" Abel asked.

"I don't need no snot-nosed little kid taking me nowhere," Sarah snarled. "I'm going to the donut shop by my own self. As for you, Abel Ruiz, you're a skinny old *bobo*, and I hate you." She turned and began walking in the direction of the donut shop.

"Estebán," Abel asked softly, "will you make sure she gets there okay?"

"Yeah, sure, man," Estebán agreed. "She's a big pain, but I'll keep an eye on her."

"Thanks, Estebán," Abel said. "You're okay, dude."

Estebán pretended he was just back riding his skateboard. But he followed Sarah until she turned on Tremayne and was at the donut shop. He watched her go in.

Meanwhile, Abel continued home. Once inside the door, the first person he saw was Penelope. "Penny, I bought you a chocolate donut," he told her. "Eat it quick before Mom sees you." Penelope was lying on the floor making a poster for her science fair project. Her report was on how the use of bleach affects cloth. It showed two contrasting swatches of material, one untouched by bleach, the other often bleached. The bleach was clearly taking its toll. She jumped up and grabbed the chocolate donut, saying, "Yesssss!"

"Penny, is there a girl in any of your classes named Sarah Suarez?" Abel asked.

With her mouth still full of donut, Penelope replied. "Yeah. She's in English with me. She's smart, but she's crazy."

"Yeah? Her mom runs the donut shop where I work," Abel told her.

"I know," Penelope responded, going back to work on her poster. "Sarah's parents got divorced when we were in seventh grade. Sarah used to be pretty nice, and we had fun sometimes. But then she got weird. She lost all her friends. They didn't want to be around her. She lied like crazy. She even lied about her parents being divorced. When her dad wasn't around anymore, Sarah said he was on a secret mission for the government in the Middle East. Then we found out the truth. Sarah got to be boy crazy after her father left. She started doing weird things and hollered at boys on the street."

Penelope paused then and looked at Abel. "I hope our parents never get divorced. They won't, I guess. Mom yells at Dad, but he never yells back."

"Yeah," Abel nodded.

"Sarah's mom is like depressed," the little sister continued. "She takes pills. Sarah said she sometimes imagines stuff. Like she'll be looking and looking for the new lipstick she bought, and it turns out she forgot to buy it. Sarah told me that. Sarah laughs about it, but I bet she's sad too."

Abel stood in the darkened hallway of his house. Maybe Elena Suarez just imagined she had a hundred dollars more than she really had.

That Saturday, Ernesto picked Abel up at ten as he promised, and they headed for the auto show. Tomás had not yet arrived at the Ruiz house, but he'd be there when Abel got back from the show.

"You know," Ernesto said as Abel got into the car, "I can't wait to unload this Volvo for something cooler. Everybody at school gives me a hard time about it. They want to know if I got it from a granny or grampa."

"It's a good car, though," Abel replied. "It always seems to run, Ernie."

"Yeah," Ernesto agreed, "that's the crazy part of it. The thing won't quit. I haven't spent anything on repairs for the car, just an oil change. It's so reliable. Mom loves it. She says she's so happy I drive a safe car. It's me and my stupid pride. I see these Mustangs and the other cool wheels, and here I am chuggin' along in the old Volvo. I mean I wouldn't even need a really cool car, just ABAV."

"What's ABAV?" Abel asked.

"Anything but a Volvo," Ernesto laughed.

"I should be at a recycling yard looking for the cruddy used crate I'm gonna buy," Abel commented.

At the show, they turned in their tickets and headed into the large auditorium filled with shiny new cars. "My parents never buy new cars," Abel remarked. "Mom says it's a sinful waste of money. We always get used cars."

"I guess that's smart," Ernesto responded. "But man, look at those beauties! Look, there's the new Ford Mustang. I've always liked that car, but they looked lame for a few years. I like the style of the new ones, though. Look at those muscle fenders, Abel. I'd love one of those babies. I can see me and Naomi riding around in that."

"Look over there," Abel pointed. "That red pickup. The Toyota Tacoma. Ernie."

The boys peered inside the pickup. "Oh man!" Ernesto exclaimed. "It's got a dual cab. It's got chrome, and, oh man, look at the V6. It's sweet."

"Ernie," Abel cried, "check out the blue LED lights in the cabin. Is that cool or what?"

"You think we'll ever be able to go in a showroom and buy a car like this, Ernie?" Abel asked. "What are the chances?"

"I don't know," Ernesto said. "Not very good, I guess. I'm thinking of being a teacher like Dad, and teachers don't make big money. Maybe Mom's picture book about the pit bull and the cat will be a sensation, and then we'll be rich. We could afford a ride like this. But I don't think Mom would buy a car like this even if she could afford it. My folks are sorta like yours, Abel. They're savers, not spenders."

"Hey, check out the Hyundai Genesis, Ernie," Abel snickered, moving to another revolving platform. A silver-colored car rotated slowly so that people could take in the entire car. "The Koreans built this." Abel peered into the cabin. "Looks upscale, but no way!"

"You know what it's got," Ernesto noted, reading the specs on the advertising poster. "It's got Bluetooth phone interface and heated seats. On a cold day you can have a warm rear end! Look at the leather. It costs a lot more than the Mustang. But a Hyundai?"

They wandered around the auditorium for another hour, admiring all the new sports cars and laughing at the old-lady cars. Then they went to the food court to buy hot dogs at inflated prices.

As they sat eating their dogs and gulping ice-cold cola, Ernesto spoke. "If we ever get to drive any of these fast cars, they'll be old when we get them. Maybe ten years old."

"I'm gonna be excited getting anything that has four wheels," Abel said. "Just so it takes me around. It's freedom, man. I'm in that house sometimes, and it's like I can feel the walls closing in around me. I just got to get outta there. Like this weekend, my brother, Tomás, he's coming in from LA. He'll be driving down today. And man my parents, especially Mom, they're gonna be making over the dude like he's the best thing that ever lived. I'd just as soon be missing in action all weekend."

"But you want to see your brother too, don't you?" Ernesto asked.

"I guess so, Ernie," Abel granted. "But we got nothing in common, you know? We got along real good when we were little. I was too young to realize he was a genius, and I'm a *bobo*."

"Come on, Abel, stop putting yourself down. You're not a *bobo*," Ernesto assured him. "Remember when Dom and Carlos were tagging and talking about dropping out of Chavez? You came up with the great idea to have them do a mural to get them interested in school again."

"Yeah," Abel admitted. "But my brother, he's so full of himself. He'll be sitting there, eating Mama's *enchiladas*. And he'll be going on and on about the top grades he's getting and about all the exciting stuff that's happening in his life. He'll be describing all the gorgeous chicks he's dating and goin' on a ski weekend. You know what, Ernie? Tomás is gonna be driving one of those big pickups or something even better. I bet anything he will be."

"Well, money isn't everything," Ernesto said. "*Abuela* is always telling us that."

"Ernie," Abel retorted, "the only people who really think money isn't important are people who have a lot of it. My dad, he's always struggled. Mom keeps reminding him that he wouldn't even have the lousy backbreaking job he has if not for the kindness of Mom's rich cousin."

Abel washed down the last of his hot dog with a big swallow of cola. "Know what, Ernie? One time I heard Mom and Tomás talking in our backyard. Was maybe when Tomás was first going off to UCLA. Mom was saying, 'Tomás, you got a great gift from God. A gift of intelligence. You're going to be an engineer. Only very smart people can be engineers. Your brother isn't smart like you, Tomás, but he's my child and I love him as much as I love you. So, Tomás, you must always remember your brother. If life does not go so well for him, you must help him, like my cousin helps your father. Promise me that, Tomás.' And Tomás, he goes, 'Yes, Mama, of course I will help him. You know that I would.'"

Abel reflected for a moment on what he'd just confided to Ernesto. Then he spoke again. "Ernie, when I heard that conversation, I was so mad I coulda screamed. I mean, I'm like sixteen years old, and they got me all figured out already. I'm gonna be a big loser like Dad. And my smart, bighearted brother is gonna maybe send over some bags of beans and rice so me and my family don't starve. I felt so humiliated, Ernie. I didn't feel like I could ever be a man."

"Yeah, I hear you," Ernesto sympathized. "I get it. If I were in your place, I'd feel the same way. But Abel, your mom is making a big mistake underestimating you. Your father too. I think she underestimated your father so much that he kinda accepted who she thought he was. He stopped trying to be the man he coulda been. I think if your mom had honored more of your father's gifts, then he might've started his own business and done well. People—even people who love you—they can pull you down bad."

Abel was silent for a few moments. Then he said, "Yeah, years and years ago I remember Dad saying he might get a little landscaping business going. He had this dream of everybody having a rock garden, a little waterfall, you know where the water recycles. But Mom said it was a crazy idea. She told him he just better go work for her cousin, where the work was steady and he could depend on a paycheck. Mom said they weren't gonna invest their little savings in some crazy scheme. Mom didn't mean to cut Dad off at the legs, but she sorta did. Now he just goes through the motions. Every day, his shoulders slump a little more."

Then Abel's eyes brightened. "When I told him how your dad admired the work he was doing on Cardinal Street, he sorta lit up for a minute. But then his eyes narrowed and he looked sad. I think it just reminded him of his dead dreams. I'm so scared that's gonna happen to me too. I'll just be a nobody."

"Abel," Ernesto insisted, grabbing his friend's shoulders and looking him directly in the eye. "That's not gonna happen to you dude. You find something you're passionate about, and you go for it. I don't care what it is. But you find it, and then you chase that dream man, with all you got. And you catch that dream and go riding on it like on a comet's tail."

Abel smiled. "You sound just like your father, Ernie. He always tells us stuff like that in class. He's a pretty calm, serious guy, quiet like, but when he starts going off preaching at us, he comes alive. Those dark eyes take fire. He leans forward, pounding his fists on the lectern, and sparks fly. Your dad, he's pretty awesome. It's like he thinks he can change the world, and sometimes I think maybe he can. He's something else, Ernie."

"Yeah," Ernesto concurred. "So, what's your dream gonna be, Abel?"

"Cooking," Abel answered.

"What?" Ernesto asked. "Did you say cooking?"

"Yeah. I sneak in the kitchen sometimes and I make stuff," Ernesto explained. "Mom laughs at me. I don't like to cook Mexican food. I like to cook French and Italian, even Thai stuff. I watch these cooks on TV, and I try to do what they do. I even went to one of those culinary schools and asked them how you get in. You know, what's the routine. I got literature from them. They give scholarships and stuff to high school seniors. I mean, I know it sounds *loco*, Ernie. But that's something I love to do more than anything. I would like to be a chef. It's *loco* but—"

"Stop it, Abel," Ernesto interrupted. "It's not *loco*. Don't do that to yourself man. Don't let anybody else do it to you either. There's good money in being a chef. If you feel passionate about it, that's a good sign it's what you're supposed to do. Don't let anybody get in the way man. I don't remember a lot about my grandfather, *Abuelo* Luis. But I remember one thing he would always say in that booming voice of his. He would say, 'Take the bull by the horns and do it!' That always stuck in my mind. Just take the bull by the horns and go for it, Abel."

Abel grinned. "You're all right, Ernie. You're really all right."

CHAPTER FIVE

You know what, Mom?" Abel said later that evening. "Next Sunday I'd like to have company over for dinner."

"Next Sunday is not a good time," Mom replied. "I have three scarves to finish, and I won't have time to go shopping and prepare a dinner for company. Some other time would be better, Abel."

"That's okay, Mom," Abel assured her. "You wouldn't be involved. I was thinking of buying all the stuff myself and making the dinner. I'd do it all, Mom. You and Dad and Penelope would just need to sit down and eat."

Mom smiled. "You're joking, of course," she said.

"No, Mom, I'm serious," Abel answered.

"Abel," Mom told him, "I know you fool around the kitchen sometimes. But you wouldn't seriously want guests to come and eat something you cooked. I mean, you're not ready for that. Who would you want to ask over anyway?"

"The Sandovals," Abel replied quickly. "Ernie's been such a good friend to me, and Mr. Sandoval is great too. He helps me out a lot at school and with problems and stuff. I thought I'd ask Ernie, his parents, and grandmother and the two little sisters over."

Mom laughed. "You want to make dinner for six guests and our family too? Abel, are you crazy?' she asked him.

"No, Mom. When you're not at home, I've done a lot of stuff in the kitchen. I watch all the cooking shows on TV. I've cooked for Aunt Marla, and she was impressed. I thought I'd make salmon," Abel explained, keeping calm in the face of Mom's disbelief. He was thinking of what Ernesto told him. He was hanging onto his dream and taking the bull by the horns.

Dad came into the kitchen to get some coffee. "What's this about salmon?" he inquired.

"Oh Sal," Mom told her husband, "this is almost too much. Abel has this absurd notion that he's going to cook dinner next Sunday for us and the whole Sandoval family, a big salmon dinner."

Abel's father looked at him. "Where did this all come from, *mi hijo*?"

"I sorta want to be a chef," Abel confessed.

"A chef!" Mom gasped. "There's never been a chef in this family. Nobody in our family ever dreamed of such a thing. Is it working at that donut shop that gave you this ridiculous idea, Abel?"

"No!" Abel protested. "I been thinking about it for a long time. I told Ernie, and he thought it was a pretty good idea, Mom. Lot of the big-time chefs are guys, you know. There's a guy from Turkey who runs a restaurant downtown, and he's making megabucks already. It's something I'm really interested in."

"Oh Abel," Mom groaned. "You're making me gray before my time. I would be so embarrassed to have the Sandovals sitting here at the table and we're serving this disaster, this horrible mess."

Abel was close to anger as he looked at his father and mother. "You guys got no faith in me at all, do you? It's always been that way. You think Tomás is some wonderful genius who can do no wrong. And I'm an idiot who is gonna screw up every time."

Abel was fuming. "I feel like just cutting out of here and going to live with Aunt Marla. She has six nieces and nephews. She told me I'm her favorite and I can stay with her anytime as long as I want. At least Aunt Marla has a little respect for me."

Abel's mother looked shocked at his tirade. "Abel," she stammered, "I do have faith in you but—"

"No you don't," Abel cut in. "It's Tomás this and Tomás that. He's like some idol around here and I'm a piece of trash. Well, I'm sick of it." Abel couldn't remember ever being angrier.

"Abel, your brother is going to be back in a few minutes," Mom announced. "He's been visiting old friends. I don't want you spoiling his visit with your bitterness."

"Oh, I won't spoil my brother's visit, Mom," Abel assured her. "Ever since he got here last night, you guys have been kneeling at his feet like he's some guru, waiting for pearls of wisdom to fall from his lips. I mean, maybe we should build a shrine to him and light candles."

Abel shocked himself by the depth of his fury. He knew he was jealous of Tomás. He had been jealous of him for a long time, but right now his feelings verged on hatred.

He didn't want that to happen, but he couldn't stem the rush of emotion.

Mom was smarter than Dad. Everybody knew that. But right now Dad seemed the wiser of the two.

"Liza," he said softly, "if the boy has his mind made up to cook dinner next Sunday and he wants his friends over, why not? It's not going to be the end of the world if it doesn't work out. We've known the Sandovals for a long time. They're just ordinary people like us. It's not like the king and queen of Spain are coming for dinner. If it turns out a little wrong, Luis and Maria Sandoval would laugh it off with us, and things'll be fine. For heavens sake, Liza, let the boy do it if he wants to."

"Sal," Mom blurted, not getting the message yet, "can you imagine the look on *Abuela* Lena's face when she sees this horrible concoction that Abel makes?"

"Liza, Liza, she'd get a kick out of it," Sal Ruiz cajoled her. "I know that woman, and she's down to earth."

The door slammed. Tomás was back from visiting his numerous friends in the *barrio*. "Now the worship begins again." Abel thought bitterly. "What delightful anecdote has the wonder boy brought to thrill his parents?" Abel caught sight of his brother in the doorway. He felt a terrible urge to punch him right in the mouth and watch those pearly white horse teeth fly all over the kitchen floor.

"Hi Tomás," Mom cooed. Then she said something that only raised Abel's rage. "Poor Abel has this ridiculous idea to cook Sunday dinner next week—salmon of all things. He wants to invite the whole Sandoval family over to join us. Can you imagine?"

Abel was stunned. Didn't Mom have a clue? Didn't she know she was just enlisting her golden boy to help demean Abel? Didn't she see how close Abel was already to loathing his older brother? Was she trying to give Abel more reason?

"Hey, I'm sorry I won't be here for that," Tomás replied. Abel listened for the sarcasm. Surely there was sarçasm. There had to be sarcasm.

But Abel didn't hear any.

"Tomás," Mom persisted, "don't you think it's a terrible idea for Abel to cook a salmon dinner and have the whole Sandoval family over? I mean, the humiliation of some fiasco—"

She didn't respect Dad, and shc didn't respect Abel. But every word from Tomás's mouth was like the gem of a prophet speaking atop a holy mountain. She waited for her wise son to confirm her fears and help spare the Ruiz family from a terrible humiliation next Sunday.

Tomás plucked an apple from the wicker basket on the dining room table and bit into it. Then he answered his mother. "I think it's a great idea, Mom. I remember when Abel and I were in middle school, we went on a hike, and Abel made the best Sloppy Joe hamburgers we'd ever had. You made fudge too, remember, Abel? It was great. I tried to make fudge a coupla times, and it always turned out chocolate pudding. Abel's fudge was to die for. Maybe Abel has a knack for cooking."

Abel stared at his brother in amazement. He remembered the fudge he'd made on the Juarez Middle School hike five years ago? Abel was stunned.

"But Tomás," Mom stammered, like the disciple of a holy man with doubts about the seer's wisdom, "fudge and hamburgers are one thing. A salmon dinner with six guests! I mean, the Sandovals will be laughing in the car all the way home. I'll be ashamed to show my face in church when they're there."

Tomás shrugged. "Chill, Mom," he advised. "Come to think of it, it was Abel who always made the pancakes on Mother's Day, remember? They were really good. Light, fluffy." Tomás turned now and looked at his younger brother. "So you want to go into cooking as a career man?"

"Maybe," Abel nodded. "A chef or something . . ."

"Cool!" Tomás affirmed. "People always want to eat good food, in boom times and bust."

"I've been sorta thinking about maybe being a chef for a long time," Abel went on, flustered by the sudden turn of events. A few moments ago he had a hard time not hating his big brother. Now his ill feeling had melted like ice on a hot sidewalk. Abel didn't know how to feel.

"Go for it, Abel," Tomás urged him. "Let me know how the salmon dinner turns out. I'll be back home again in a few weeks for my birthday. You gotta make dinner for me then." He looked at his phone. "Gotta go again. Lotta guys want to see me in the old *barrio*." Then he was out the door.

"Well . . . ," Mom spoke slowly after Tomás left. "I'm going to be busy next weekend, but I'll help you all I can, Abel."

"No Mom," Abel insisted. "I don't want any help. That would ruin everything. It wouldn't be my gig then. I want to do it all myself."

Liza Ruiz looked at her husband with a gesture of frustration.

All week Abel thought about the salmon dinner he was going to prepare on Sunday. He wasn't nervous about making it. He was just excited. A few times, when he had stayed over at Aunt Marla's house, he had made dinner for himself and his aunt. He made chicken manicotti one night. Right after that dinner, Aunt Marla told Abel he was welcome to come stay with her as often and as long as he liked. She wasn't, she explained with a chuckle, a very good cook.

Abel had never confided his dream of being a chef to anyone until the other day when he told Ernesto. He was always afraid people would laugh, but he felt so close to Ernesto that he just blurted it out. Ernesto's pep talk about following his dreams gave him the courage to open up.

At school on Monday, Abel couldn't wait for lunch so that he could invite

Ernesto and his family to Sunday dinner in person. Texting him about it just didn't seem cool. A Sunday salmon dinner was too special to send the invitation by cell phone. The minute Ernesto walked up, Abel said abruptly, "Hey man, how about you and your family coming to my house for a salmon dinner on Sunday? I'm cooking it."

Ernesto grinned. "Listen man, I never turn down a free dinner. You mean we can all come, even *Abuela* and my sisters?" Ernesto asked.

"Yeah. I sprung it on my mom, and she went nuts," Abel told him. "She didn't think I could do it. She freaked man. She doesn't think I can do anything, but then a real weird thing happened. In comes my wonderful brother, who can do no wrong. Mom asks him if my plan to make dinner isn't the stupidest thing he ever heard of. Tomás blows my mind by siding with *me*! It was like a miracle, Ernie. Took the wind right outta Mom's sails."

Monday afternoon went well at the donut shop. Elena didn't talk about any more missing money. And Paul, Claudia, and Abel handled the brisk business. Abel was starting to feel more optimistic.

At about five-thirty, Abel went into the back room for more jelly donuts. Elena had gone home, and he needed to add to the display case. Paul was outside in the parking lot talking to someone on his cell phone. Abel didn't mean to eavesdrop. But Paul was talking in a loud, agitated voice, and he couldn't help overhearing.

"I'll have it for you tomorrow," Paul was saying. "Tomorrow, okay? . . . Yeah, I got the money. I swear I got it, man. I'm not trying to stiff you, okay?"

Abel hurried back into the front of the store. He didn't want Paul to know he had heard anything. Abel felt numb. Paul sounded as though he was trying to calm somebody down, somebody he owed money to. Maybe the call wasn't about that at all, but it sure sounded like it. A terrible thought crossed Abel's mind. Maybe Paul was hammered for money, and he *did* rob the till. Maybe Elena wasn't imagining things at all. But if that happened, then all the crew would be under suspicion, including Abel.

When Paul came back inside, he looked upset. Claudia asked, "You okay, Paul?"

"Yeah, fine, great. Why?" Paul snapped. He started to resupply the coffee station with sugar and napkins. Claudia exchanged a look with Abel. When Paul got off his shift, he sprinted out of the shop, got into his car, and left a lot of rubber in the street in his getaway.

"What's that all about?" Abel asked Claudia.

"I don't know," Claudia responded. "He got a call on his cell and went out to talk. Paul gambles. I think somebody is pressing him over a gambling debt. I hate gambling. It's like setting fire to your money."

Abel thought to himself, "Please don't let there be any money missing tonight when Elena checks the receipts."

The rest of that week, when Abel worked at the donut shop, Elena seemed even more distracted than usual. Everybody was on edge. Once she couldn't locate ten dollars she was sure she had put into her purse. For a few minutes Abel was nervous. She always left her purse in a drawer in the back room, and nobody went in there but Elena and the crew. Elena said she thought her purse was safe there, but maybe not. She was getting closer to starting to accuse somebody.

After that incident, Paul Morales gave Abel and Claudia a knowing look. "She's cracking up, you guys," he advised. "Mark my words. This is gonna have a bad ending."

"Oh Paul," Claudia protested, "don't be silly."

Abel thought about Sarah Suarez, Elena's daughter, and he figured it was no wonder the poor woman was losing it. To have a daughter like that, an eighteen-year-old wacko beauty queen in the body of a thirteen-year-old had to be horrible.

Toward the end of the week, Abel's preparations for his big dinner became more intense. He planned to make a lemon dill salmon with small red potatoes, along with a leafy green salad with tiny tomatoes. He was going all out for dessert, making a banana cream trifle ahead of time and storing it in the refrigerator. (He'd checked the pantry in the kitchen, and there was just enough sherry for his recipe.)

Abel went to the supermarket on Saturday to get everything he needed. As he shopped, his excitement grew by leaps and bounds. He couldn't remember many occasions in his life that he had done something to impress his parents, and he was eager to do that. He got so-so report cards and did blah science fair projects. Now, finally, he was making a big splash. His parents were going to be amazed. Neither his mother nor his father expected anything but a dismal failure. Penelope wasn't sure what was going to happen, but she had picked up on her parent's low assessment of Abel's abilities. While Abel was getting dinner ready on Sunday, Penelope came out to the kitchen and stared at him suspiciously. Finally, she said, "Do you *really* know how to do this, Abel?"

"I sure do," Abel replied with a smile. Abel was exulting ahead of time how bowled over everybody would be by his dinner.

The next day, Sunday, the Sandovals arrived at the Ruiz home. When they came in, Abel's mother and father greeted them warmly. Abel heard Mom say to Ernesto's mother, "I must warn you. Our son Abel is doing this entire dinner, and he hasn't ever done anything like this before. So I hope it's okay. Just in case, we've got the phone number for the pizzeria ready." Mrs. Ruiz laughed shakily.

"Oh, I bet it'll be wonderful," Maria Sandoval responded.

"Yeah," Ernesto added. "I know it'll be. I can hardly wait. I'm crazy about salmon."

Penelope appeared behind her parents. "Hi," she said. "My crazy brother is making dinner. You guys might as well sit down."

When the Sandovals and Abel's family were seated at the table, which had been made larger with extenders, Abel appeared with the salad. It had small bunches of romaine, tomatoes, freshly grated parmesan cheese, ground pepper, and homemade caesar dressing. Abel wore a nice white shirt and tie. He looked like a real waiter.

"Abel," Maria Sandoval commented, "you look so handsome."

Abel smiled and nodded to Luis Sandoval, his teacher, and to the rest of the family. "It's real nice to see everybody," he told them. "I hope everything is okay."

"Don't count on it," Penelope warned. Her mother kicked her under the table.

Abel didn't join the others as they ate their salads. He was too busy preparing the plates for the main course. He had sprinkled the salmon fillets with lemon pepper and cooked them in olive oil. He cooked the small red potatoes, then added bacon pieces. Just before serving the salmon, he added lemon juice, dill weed, and more lemon pepper.

When the salad plates were taken away and the salmon served to everyone, Abel took his seat at the table. He then said something he'd heard the chefs say on some of the cooking shows.

"Enjoy!" he said to everyone. The two families dug into Abel's meal. Everyone was silent for what seemed to Abel like a long time. Then Maria Sandoval was the first to speak

"Oh my!" she exclaimed. "This is delicious!"

"Remember when we splurged at that nice restaurant downtown and had salmon," Luis Sandoval recalled. "It wasn't anything to compare with this. This is so flaky and tender."

Eight-year-old Katalina chimed in. "Abel, you gotta come to our house and cook sometimes. *Abuela* is a good cook, and Mom is okay, but I never tasted something like this."

Abuela Lena looked at Abel and asked, "Where did you learn to cook like this, Abel? Have you taken lessons?"

"No, Mrs. Sandoval," Abel answered. "I watch the guys on TV, and I read a lot of cookbooks. I've tried out stuff a lot at my Aunt Marla's condo. I really love to cook. I mean, it just pulls me into a zone like. It's almost like art."

"Well, it *is* art," *Abuela* agreed. "I think it is one of the world's greatest forms of art because eating is such a joyous thing."

Their salmon finished, the diners sat and chatted while Abel took the dishes away. When everyone had had time to digest the meal, Penelope helped Abel bring in the banana cream trifles. The dessert was a perfect end to the meal.

Luis Sandoval leaned back in his chair and looked at Abel. "The meal was amazing, Abel," he declared. "I bet there's not another sixteen-year-old kid in the county who could have pulled off something like this. If you want a career in cooking, you're well on the way."

Ernesto's father glanced at Liza Ruiz. "You must be some great cook too, Liza. Abel must have learned a lot at your side."

Liza Ruiz looked flustered as she responded. "Uh well . . . I'm all right as a cook, but I never dreamed Abel was into cooking like this. So I didn't spend much time teaching him anything."

"To tell the truth, Luis," Sal Ruiz added, "we never knew Abel liked to cook at all. Abel's never been much good at anything. He's sorta like me. Just a nice kid who sorta blunders along. Our other kid, Tomás, now he's a genius. Everything he touches turns to gold, but Abel . . ."

The man's voice trailed off. He saw the hurt in his younger son's eyes. He wanted to say something that would ease the pain his words had caused, but he was too late. What he had said he could not recall. So Sal Ruiz finished his banana cream trifle in silence.

"You know what?" Penelope piped up as she helped Abel clear the table. "That was the most awesome dinner I ever had in this house. I thought it'd be horrible, Abel. I don't even like fish, and I *loved* it."

Abel smiled at his sister, "Thanks, Penny," he told her.

The Sandovals and the Ruizes then went into the living room for coffee and hot chocolate. The moms and dads talked about things in general. The girls played a game on the computer. And Ernie helped Abel clean up in the kitchen.

When it was time to go, the Sandovals thanked Abel and his parents for asking them over and for the wonderful dinner. The last of the Sandovals out the door was Ernesto. He and Abel high-fived and fist-bumped. "It was a home run, man," Ernesto assured his friend.

Abel closed the door, flushed with happiness. He expected his meal to turn out well. He had experimented with many meals at Aunt Marla's condo. He had read many books. He had watched the TV cooking shows. He was certain he was going to pull it off.

But now, with the Sandovals gone, his parents looked at Abel with nothing short of astonishment.

They had been sure he would fail, just as he failed at everything else. They were sure of it.

"You did great, *muchacho*!" his father announced. Abel thought he saw tears in the man's eyes.

CHAPTER SIX

At Elena's donut shop on Monday afternoon, the woman was talking to herself in the back room. "This is just too much!" she cried. She came out to where Paul Morales and Abel were at the counter. Claudia hadn't arrived yet. "There's sixty dollars missing from my purse," she stormed. "I know I put sixty dollars in my purse this morning before I left the house. Now there's like a dollar and some change in there!"

Paul tried to reason with her. "Elena, you've been working back there the whole time you've been here. You woulda seen somebody come in and—"

"But I went to the bathroom," Elena countered. "Anything could have happened while I was in there!" Her dark eyes pierced Abel and Paul like lasers. "I make little enough profit here without being robbed by my own employees!"

Abel felt like he'd just been hit in the stomach with a sand bag. He got an instant, blinding headache. "Elena," he declared. "I'd never take money from somebody's purse. I wouldn't do that in a million years!"

"I didn't touch your purse either, Elena," Paul asserted. "I been out here the whole time waiting on customers. I didn't even see you go in the bathroom. I thought you were sitting at your desk the whole time, probably with your purse right next to you. You think I'd go in that back room and try to steal something with you sitting right there?"

"I'm not crazy," Elena Suarez fumed. "I put sixty dollars in the purse this morning because I was going to get my hair done. I put in three twenties before I left the house. Now they're gone!"

Abel thought if he got any sicker, he'd upchuck. Some customers came in, and he and Paul waited on them. Then Claudia arrived. She noticed the tense atmosphere, and she looked around nervously. "What's the matter?" Claudia asked. "What happened?"

"Somebody stole sixty dollars from my purse, that's what happened," Elena stated bitterly.

"*What*?" Claudia gasped. "You think somebody came in that back door and rifled your purse?"

"The back door was locked," Elena answered coldly. She narrowed her eyes and glared at the two boys at the counter. "I don't want to make trouble for you kids," she advised. "I like you both. I know things come up. Maybe you need money right away, and you think you'll pay it back later on . . ."

"I didn't take the money," Abel stammered. "I wasn't raised that way. I never stole from anybody in my life." Abel was terrified by the thought that he might be in serious trouble, even though he didn't do anything wrong. He'd been so happy since the dinner the day before. He'd been riding high. For the first time in his life, he had done something grand that made his parents proud of him. If Abel was arrested on suspicion of theft, his family would be devastated. He would be the first person in his family ever to get in trouble with the law. Abel couldn't take it.

"One of you boys took the money from my purse," Elena Suarez accused them. "What're you trying to say? That you both stepped outside and some customer rushed into the back room and robbed me? But nobody knows I keep my purse in that top desk drawer except you guys. I'm very sorry to be doing this. But I want both of you to come in the back room and hand me your wallets so I can check them. My three twenties were crisp brand new bills. I'm sure I'll recognize them." She turned to Claudia. "Take over the counter,

Claudia, while we settle this once and for all."

A look of horror came over Claudia's face. "Elena, this is ridiculous," she objected.

In the back room, Paul Morales handed Elena his wallet. He had a crinkled five dollar bill and some change. Then Abel did the same. He had just change. He'd spent most of his cash on the Sunday dinner. He was waiting eagerly for his pay to replenish his cash.

"Turn your pockets inside out," Elena commanded.

Both boys complied. Abel's pockets contained nothing but lint and some sales slips. Paul's had a movie ticket stub.

"One of you has hidden the money somewhere," Elena decided darkly. Abel wondered what was coming next, a strip search?

"Lady," Paul exploded, "I got a good mind to go out there in front and yank open the display case and toss all your stinking donuts all over the floor. You've humiliated us, and we didn't do anything. You want to know what I think? I think you're a crazy old lady and belong in a nut house."

Paul stomped over to where his jacket was hanging on a peg, got it, and put it on. "I'm not working here anymore, lady. You drove your husband away. Now you're making this stinking job so bad that I'm being treated like a common criminal when I didn't do anything. And don't get any ideas about calling the cops on me and sending them to my door. I got friends, lady. I got homies who got my back. If you try to make trouble for me, you'll be the sorriest old *bruja* in the *barrio*!" Paul turned sharply and went out the back door to his car.

Elena Suarez watched him go. She shook her head as she spoke. "It had to be him, and the way he acted proves it. I had a feeling it was him. He took the money. He was probably hiding it in his socks or something. He gambles. He has debts."

She turned and looked at Abel, smiling thinly. "I never really suspected you, Abel. I had to make you hand over your wallet and empty your pockets too. I didn't want him to think I was singling him out. But I know you're a good boy, Abel. I've had misgivings about Paul for a long time. I've seen him on the street with those awful boys with shaved heads."

Abel's head was spinning. Customers were coming in, and he joined Claudia at the counter. They wanted chocolate and glazed donuts and bear claws and apple fritters. Some wanted powdered sugar donuts and coffee. Whatever the customers asked for, Abel worked like a robot, with Claudia beside him. He didn't believe Paul was guilty of anything. He didn't care if he hung with homies. A lot of good kids did. Dom Reynosa and Carlos Negrete did, and they were good guys. Elena was being evil and unfair in accusing Paul of stealing her money.

Abel felt as though he was in a trance. The donut shop was busy for about an hour;

then things quieted down. Elena Suarez went off to the ATM machine to get more money so that she could get her hair done.

"You think she's gonna call the cops on Paul?" Abel asked Claudia.

"I don't think so . . . maybe," Claudia sighed. "She has no proof. But she could get the police to hassle him. Sometimes they hassle kids just on a tip. I hope not. She's done enough to the poor guy."

Abel turned and looked at Claudia. "What do you think happened to the money?" he asked her.

"She probably left it at home," Claudia replied bitterly.

Abel remembered Paul's frantic phone call in the parking lot when he was trying to hold off a debtor. "You don't think Paul woulda taken it, do you?" he asked Claudia.

"No," Claudia answered. "I feel so sorry for Paul. He's been in a little trouble before, but he's straightened out his act. He's a good, bright guy. He's in technical school, and he's got a good future. I don't want this stupid thing to derail him. This is so rotten. Elena is in a fog half the time. She loses stuff all the time."

Claudia was silent while she wiped off the counter. Then she began speaking again. "I don't feel like working here myself anymore. Now that Paul's gone, whenever she misplaces money, we'll be on the spot. Abel, I feel like quitting, but I need the job. I need the money to help my parents with my tuition. I love my school. I'd feel terrible if I had to drop out in my junior year and not graduate next year with my friends." Claudia seemed close to tears.

"I feel the same way," Abel concurred. "I'd like to quit right now. I would if I was sure I could get another job. But the hardware store just closed, and so did the chicken place. Lotta stores've closed down. Jobs are kinda scarce right now. I'm saving money for a car. And now I can do things like that Sunday dinner I made for my family and my friends. I feel better about myself than I've ever felt before."

"I'm just so scared she'll come after us, Abel," Claudia said.

Abel took a deep breath. "Claudia, let's look out for each other. I won't ever go in the back room unless we go together, and you do the same. Let's have each other's backs every minute. If she accuses one of us, then we can vouch for each other."

"This is so rotten," Claudia declared. "I almost hate Elena. Isn't that terrible? In my school, they're all the time harping on love one another. But I'm having a hard time not hating that woman. But you're right, Abel. We can stick together and make it through. We can."

When Elena Suarez returned from the ATM machine, she looked at Abel and Claudia. Then she said with a self-satisfied smirk, "Well, don't we all feel a lot safer around here now that that thief is gone?"

Claudia looked at Abel. She seemed to expect him to say something. When he didn't, Claudia spoke up. "Elena, I don't think Paul Morales is a thief. I don't think he took your money. I feel really bad about what happened. But Abel and I, we both feel threatened now. I think you better lock your purse in that desk drawer when you leave it so nobody can possibly get in. I think you need to check and recheck the receipts. I think you've got a lot on your plate, Elena, with stuff at home. I think maybe you're nervous and you misplace stuff. Abel and I don't want to be accused of anything."

"I trust you, Claudia," Elena Suarez assured her. "And I trust Abel too. I always thought Paul was a shifty guy, but he was so good at the counter that I kept him. But if it will make you feel better, I'll do as you say. My purse will always be in a locked drawer, and I'll be very vigilant about the receipts. Then there won't be any problems."

When Elena went into the back room, Abel turned to Claudia. "That was good,

Claudia. That took a lot of courage. I know I let you down. I should've said that."

"No Abel," Claudia told him, "you're new here. I've worked for Elena for months. I was the better one to say it. I'm really ticked off at that woman. She gave Paul a raw deal."

Abel wondered whether Claudia liked Paul more than she was saying. Maybe even they were girlfriend and boyfriend. "Uh, Claudia, is Paul a real good friend of yours?" he asked.

"Not really," the girl answered. "We both started to work here at about the same time. He was always nice to me. He's a good guy. I hate what that woman did."

During the next lull in business, Abel worked up the courage to ask Claudia something he'd been thinking about ever since he started working at the shop. "Uh, Claudia, you got a steady boyfriend?"

"No," she explained. "I go to an all-girls school, you know. We get together with boys from an all-boys school sometimes, but it's kinda hard to form relationships. My parents are real strict, Abel. Lotta girls in the *barrio* get in trouble, you know. And my parents didn't want that to happen to me. I respect that. I've never been a wild child. I'm kinda dull, Abel."

"I don't think you're dull, Claudia," Abel told her, warmly. "I think you're really . . . great. If you didn't have anything better to do after work some day, maybe we could go down and have a frozen yogurt or something."

"Yeah, that'd be nice!" Claudia said excitedly. "I've gotten turned off of donuts since I've been working here. But a frozen yogurt on a muggy day like today sounds good."

"Good," Abel confirmed, his heart beating fast. "So after work we'll stop at the yogurt shop. I go past it on my way home. I live on Sparrow Street. Where do you live?"

"Wren Street," Claudia said.

"Oh, that's where my best friend, Ernesto lives," Abel told her. "After we have our yogurts, I'll walk you home, Claudia.

As Claudia and Abel were getting ready to go home, Elena Suarez was very cordial. She apologized again for making Abel turn over his wallet and empty his pockets. "I'm so glad you're working here, Abel," she assured him. "I'll get someone to replace Paul, but you two—you and Claudia—are just so good."

Abel and Claudia were both sickened by the woman's gushing, but neither of them said anything. They quietly got their jackets and headed for the frozen yogurt place. Once they were far enough away from the store, Claudia said, "Elena seems to feel a little guilty about everything. But a lot of good that does poor Paul!" Abel silently agreed.

On the way to the store, as they started down Tremayne Street, Abel saw Sarah Suarez and two girls coming in the opposite direction. As they passed each other, Sarah sang out loudly enough to be overheard.

"Look, there's old four-eyes, otherwise known as the wicked witch of the west, with that cute Abel Ruiz. What a shame!"

"Go stuff an apple fritter in your mouth, Sarah," Claudia told her. Sarah glared at them and headed for her mother's shop.

At the yogurt store, Claudia bought a strawberry yogurt and Abel bought a chocolate one. Abel talked about his Sunday dinner and what a big hit it was. "My parents never saw me do anything like that before. Their jaws just dropped, Claudia. It was so cool."

"That's wonderful, Abel," Claudia affirmed, a big smile on her face. "Good for you that you attempted something like that. I mean, that's a big deal. A salmon dinner and having guests over too." She looked really beautiful to Abel when she smiled.

"I got this brother who goes to UCLA," Abel continued, "and everything he does is right. My parents just worship him. Anyway, my friend, Ernesto, he and I went to the car show Saturday. We got to talking.

113

Ernie, he said you gotta find something you're passionate about, and just go for it. Well, for me it's cooking. And what Ernie said, it gave me the courage to dream up that dinner. What made it really cool was that I invited Ernie and his whole family—six of them. So I cooked dinner for ten people Sunday. I'm telling you, Claudia, usually I feel like about two cents. But after that dinner coming off so good, I felt like a million bucks."

Claudia was looking intently at Abel. "That's beautiful, Abel. That's really beautiful. Your friend is right. You gotta find that one thing that you really care about and go for it. It's an awful thing to spend your whole life doing a job you hate. And the only reason is 'cause that's the first place that hired you when you finished school."

"Yeah," Abel agreed, wondering whether Claudia was really excited about anything.

"My dad's a salesman," Claudia went on. "He sells insurance. Mostly life insurance.

114

He earns a good living, but he hates the job. He always told me the last thing he ever wanted to do was be a salesman. It's almost like a prison sentence. He was sentenced to be a salesman until he can retire and get his Social Security check or something."

The girl took another spoonful of her strawberry yogurt. "Mmm, good! Anyway, when Dad was young, he surfed. He loved the ocean. He had this idea he might open up a surfboard shop on the beach. Then he met Mom, and they fell in love. Mom's dad called him 'a surfer bum.' Dad quickly got a nice respectable job selling insurance, and that was that. It's not that Dad isn't happy. I mean, he's happy. He and Mom love each other a lot. And when he does retire, they're gonna get a little beach cottage. So Dad can sorta enjoy that life again. But still . . . I mean, Abel, your friend, he's got it right. You need to do a job that makes you happy. You shouldn't just settle for the paycheck."

It was getting late when Claudia and Abel started down Tremayne for the walk home.

Abel told Claudia about his dad. "My dad wanted to build brick walls and little ponds and waterfalls, but it didn't happen that way. He got hired by Mom's cousin, and now mostly he hauls sand and gravel around."

Claudia nodded. Abel wondered again whether she had a secret dream. He wished he knew how to ask her without seeming to be nosy and prying into her life. They hadn't known each other very long.

"Abel, do you like English?" Claudia asked.

"No, not really," Abel confessed. "I don't understand a lot of the stories we're reading in English. They're kind of boring too. The teacher keeps wanting to know what the story means, and to me it doesn't mean anything. Like we're reading this thing by Hemingway, 'A Canary for One,' and it makes no sense to me. A lot of the stories in English make no sense to me. I guess I'm not very good in English. I'm lucky if I get a B minus. Usually I get a C plus. Now Ernie, he's a pretty good student. I'm gonna ask him what that canary story means. He'll know."

"I love poetry that was written a long time ago," Claudia responded. "And essays too. I like the stuff Henry David Thoreau wrote. When we were talking about our dads, I thought about something Thoreau wrote, and it kinda fit. He wrote, 'The mass of men lead lives of quiet desperation.' Isn't that true? But it's sad too."

They were getting close to their homes. If he was going to ask Claudia about her secret passion for a career, he figured now was the time. "Claudia," he began, "you ever think about what you want to do when you finish school? I mean, you'll probably want to go to college, but then . . . ?"

Claudia giggled. "Mine is stranger than you wanting to be a chef, Abel."

"Yeah?" Abel smiled. "Tell me."

"We do musical comedies at our school," Claudia explained, a bright glow in her beautiful brown eyes. "The boys come to play the male parts. I've been in several of the musicals. I got a nice voice. I'm sort of a soprano. I'd like to take music and maybe sing, Abel."

When they got to Claudia's house, she stopped before going inside. "Abel," she said, taking his big hands in her small ones. "Let's promise each other that we'll never lead lives of quiet desperation."

CHAPTER SEVEN

When Abel got home from school on Tuesday, Penelope was just coming in too. She flopped down in front of the television set and reached into her backpack for a huge apple fritter. The fritter was on its way toward her mouth when Mom came into the room.

"Penelope Ruiz!" Mom screamed. "What are you doing? We're having dinner in a couple of hours, and you're stuffing yourself with some unhealthy, greasy apple fritter!" Mom's wrath quickly refocused on Abel.

"Abel, shame on you, bringing that junk home when you know your sister shouldn't be eating that stuff!"

"Mom," Abel explained patiently, "I didn't bring the apple fritter home. I don't bring anything home from that place. It makes me sick just looking at it."

Mom grabbed Penelope's backpack and cried, "This is full of disgusting greasy pastries, bear claws, hideous glazed donuts. Penelope, what is going on? You *know* you're putting on too much weight and this garbage isn't good for you. Where did you get all this stuff? Did you spend your whole week's allowance in one day?"

"I didn't buy any of it," Penelope answered. "A girl at school was passing them all out. She was giving stuff to all the girls. And I am *not* putting on weight. Stop saying that, Mom. You want me to be one of those horrible skinny girls who don't eat *anything*?"

Mom snatched all the pastries and dumped them into the garbage bag in the kitchen. Both kids heard her comment from the kitchen. "These are going out where they belong, in the trash."

"Mommm," Penelope wailed. "You could at least give them to the poor at that Father Joe's Village."

"The poor don't deserve this kind of greasy garbage either," Mom declared, coming back to the living room, backpack in hand. "Shame on that girl passing out stuff like this. She shouldn't be giving junk food away to the children. Doesn't she realize the obesity problem in this country—in the *barrio*! Does she want to give all the kids diabetes and heart trouble? Who is this girl anyway? Is she one of your friends, Penelope?"

"No," Penelope sighed. "Her mom owns the donut shop where Abel works."

"Sarah?" Abel commented. "She's kinda weird."

"Yeah," Penelope agreed. "She doesn't have many friends 'cause she acts older than everybody else. I guess she thought we'd like her better if she gave us all this stuff."

Abel grimaced. "Know what, Mom? Elena Suarez, Sarah's mother, she's kind of a scatterbrain. It's no wonder the kid is weird."

Abel was dying to tell his mother the whole sad story. He wanted to talk about how Elena accused him and Paul of stealing her sixty dollars, how she made them give her their wallets and empty their pockets. He wanted to talk to his mother, but he didn't dare. She'd get so upset she'd demand that he quit his job at once. And he didn't want to do that. Making money was too good. Mom was pretty stingy with the money she gave Abel. Before he got his job, he wouldn't have even been able to pay for Claudia's frozen yogurt. So Abel didn't dare talk about what happened at the donut shop.

Mom then sat down at her work area in the living room. She wanted to finish the scarves she was working on before making dinner.

Penelope walked over to where Abel was working on the computer and whispered, "Sarah uses weed, Abel."

Abel looked up. "You sure?" he asked her in a very quiet tone.

"Yeah, she had this weird little cigarette. She offered us all a drag on it," Penelope explained. They were speaking in hushed voices, like convicts in prison.

"You didn't try it, did you?" Abel asked. Penelope often annoyed Abel, but she was his little sister and he loved her. He didn't want her to get into trouble.

"No, I was scared to," Penelope answered. "I was scared Mom would find out and kill me. I mean, not really kill me. But you know what I mean. You're kind of scared of Mom too, aren't you? I know Dad is."

"Yeah," Abel admitted, "we're all a little scared of Mom. She's a real strong woman. But she loves us, and she wants what's best for us. And smoking dope isn't good for anybody. You smoke dope, and the next thing you know, you're in bigger trouble."

Abel wanted to drive the point home with his sister. "The other night I saw cop cars at the Costa house down the street. Their kids been smoking dope. Now I saw the cops take one of them away in handcuffs. The mom and dad were standing there crying. I don't know what the dude did. But I've seen him at Chavez smoking dope. Maybe they caught him dealing. The kid's a sophomore. It looked weird seeing him in handcuffs, Penelope. I think the kid was crying too. His hair was all messy, like the cops just got him out of bed."

Apparently, Penelope was only half listening. She asked, "Abel, tell me the truth. Am I fat?"

Abel laughed. "No, you're not fat, Penny. But you could be if you keep eating too many apple fritters."

On Wednesday, Abel and Claudia were working the counter with a new kid Elena had just hired. His name was Zeno. Abel couldn't believe he was breaking Zeno in, just as Paul broke him in a few weeks ago.

Zeno seemed to be a nice kid and catching on quickly. Abel didn't know whether he should feel sorry for the kid. Would Elena pounce on him eventually with one of her accusations? Abel didn't have to wait long to find out.

Elena came from the back room with a concerned look on her face. "Zeno, when I hired you, I made it clear, didn't I. You were not free to take any of the merchandise without paying for it."

"What?" Zeno asked.

"You can't take donuts home free," Elena explained. "You know employees aren't allowed to do that. I thought I'd explained that, but maybe I didn't."

"Uh, no ma'am, you didn't say anything about that," Zeno responded. "But I knew that already. I worked at a hamburger place, and I never took no hamburgers home without paying for them. Why would anybody do that?"

"Well, there was a tray of donuts and bear claws and apple fritters in the back, waiting to go into the display case," Elena explained. "Now they've disappeared. I thought perhaps you took them yesterday and put them in your car to take home."

"No ma'am, I didn't," a deeply perplexed Zeno asserted. "I wouldn't think of doing that. He glanced at Abel and Claudia who shrugged sympathetically.

"Well, they didn't walk off by themselves," Elena snapped.

The explanation then dawned on Abel. He remembered Penelope bringing home all those sweets from school yesterday.

"Elena," Abel spoke up. "I think I know what happened to that tray of sweets."

"Oh my goodness, Abel," Elena exclaimed, "did you take them? But you didn't even work yesterday, and it was Zeno's first day. I don't understand."

"My sister, Penelope," Abel explained, "she goes to middle school with your daughter, Sarah. Yesterday Penny brought home an apple fritter and other stuff, and Mom got mad. Penny said Sarah brought a whole bunch of bakery stuff to school and was passing it out to all the girls. So, what I think happened is, Sarah came in here yesterday on her way to school and sorta made off with the tray."

"Sarah would never—" Elena stammered. "She knows better than to take bakery goods from here. She did it once before. And I'm not ashamed to tell you that I took the hair brush to that girl, and she couldn't sit down comfortably for a few days. Well, I'll just see about this. I am really disappointed if Sarah took the tray." Elena disappeared into the back room, flushed with embarrassment.

"Wow!" Zeno said. "She had me going for a minute there."

"Elena is always accusing the employees of stuff, Zeno," Claudia warned him. "That's why we gotta watch out for each other. Nobody goes in that back room alone, and we all stick together."

Zeno nodded. "Thanks Claudia," he acknowledged.

After work, Claudia and Abel walked home together again. Abel just walked Claudia to Wren Street and then kept going to Sparrow, where he lived. The walk gave Abel a wonderful opportunity to get to know Claudia better, to get closer to her.

"I've got about a thousand dollars in the bank now," Abel announced. "Ernie and me, we're huntin' on the Internet for bargains. I don't care what kind of a car it is, as long as it runs good like Ernie's Volvo. I won't be able to afford repair bills. I'm real antsy for a car now."

"I think you could get something pretty good for a thousand," Claudia noted. "Probably wouldn't look like much, but it'd run."

"Mom doesn't want me to get a car," Abel commented. "She thinks I'm too dumb to drive good. She thinks I'll have an accident and make trouble for the family. Mom thinks I can't do much of anything, but she's still pretty amazed by that Sunday dinner. I think she wonders if I used magic dust or something."

"What about your dad?" Claudia asked. "I bet he'd like for you to have a car. Dads like to talk cars with their sons."

"Dad just parrots what Mom wants," Abel responded. "Dad likes peace, and you don't have any peace in our house if you argue with Mom. But the thing is, I think about the car all the time. I wake up thinking about it, and I go to bed at night thinking about it. Sometimes I dream I bought it already and I'm driving it around town. Those are good dreams."

As they walked down Tremayne, Abel and Claudia saw Paul Morales with some of his friends, his homies. Paul wore a white T-shirt and jeans, but the other boys were in baggy clothing. Paul had a nice head of curly black hair. But two of the homies had their heads shaved and tattoos on the sides of their heads. If a police cruiser came by, the cops would probably think this group of dudes was getting ready to rob a store or make a drug deal. But all they were doing was drinking beer.

"Hey Paul," Abel called out.

Paul turned. "Hey man. Hey Claudia. The old *bruja* still accusing people?" he asked.

"Yeah," Abel replied. "We got a new kid—Zeno. He started working yesterday. She was already accusing him of ripping off a tray of donuts and fritters. Luckily I knew what happened to the stuff. Sarah, her kid, stole it and was passing it out to the girls in the middle school."

"We're really sorry about what happened, Paul," Claudia told him. "We miss you down there. It's not the same without you. Abel and me would like to walk out too, but we need our jobs so bad."

"Well, what goes around comes around," Paul responded. "She'll get hers. You can't treat people like she does and get away with it forever. One of these days payback time will come."

Claudia and Abel walked on, turning down Wren Street. They noticed a girl coming toward them in the dark.

130

"Oh no!" Abel groaned. "Oh brother! Is that Sarah Suarez?"

"I'm afraid it is," Claudia confirmed. "And it's too late to be going to the donut shop. Elena is closed. What's she roaming around the streets for at this hour?"

"Do you know where she lives, Claudia?" Abel asked.

"Yeah, she and her mother live in a condo over on Cardinal Street," Claudia answered.

"My Aunt Marla lives on that street," Abel said. As they drew closer to the girl, Claudia called out, "Where are you going, Sarah?"

"None of your business, four-eyes," Sarah snapped.

"You shouldn't be out here by yourself, girl," Abel advised.

"Your stupid sister ratted me out," Sarah snarled bitterly. "I was trying to be nice to those girls. I gave them all those goodies. I don't know what the big deal was. The stuff was kinda stale anyway. But

Penny told you and you told my mom. Abel Ruiz, you're a rat. Mom got all bent out of shape about it. She went on and on about me stealing her stupid apple fritters. I hate her. I hate her so much."

Sarah's voice trembled a little in spite of her bravado. "My dad was nice. He loves me a lot. But she doesn't care about me. If you care about somebody, you don't beat them with a hairbrush."

"Sarah," Claudia advised, "you need to go home now."

"I don't need to do anything I don't want to do," Sarah snapped back.

Claudia took out her cell phone. "I'm calling your mother to come get you. Cardinal Street is way down at the end of Tremayne, and it's dark. It's dangerous out here."

"My boyfriend is meeting me," Sarah objected. "He'll take me home. He has a red Mustang."

"What kind of a boyfriend does a thirteen-year-old girl have?" Abel asked her. "No guy old enough to drive a car is gonna want a middle schooler for a girl-friend. You're lying again, Sarah. You're making it up. You got no boyfriend."

"I have Elena's number," Claudia said, waiting for her call to be answered.

"Hi," Elena Suarez said in a slurred voice. "Who's this?"

"Elena, this is Claudia. I'm out here on Tremayne Street, and Sarah is wandering around by herself. I think you need to come get her, okay?"

"Sarah isn't on the street," Elena asserted. Her voice sounded very thick. "She's home in bed, Claudia. I made her go to bed early. I punished her for stealing the bakery goods. I punished her good. She was crying her eyes out, but now she's in bed sleeping."

As she listened to Elena, Claudia whispered to Abel, "She sounds buzzed." Then Claudia spoke again to Elena. "You better go check Sarah's room. You'll see she's not there."

"I'm telling you," Elena insisted, "she's in her bed sleeping. I gotta go now. I got a headache. You woke me up for nothing, and now I'm going back to bed." Elena hung up the phone.

"She's been drinking all night," Sarah declared. "She drinks a lot, and she takes pills too. That's why she forgets stuff. She leaves money laying around. It drops to the floor, and the cat plays with it. My Uncle Hector, he set her up in that donut shop. But she doesn't know what she's doing."

Abel noted that they were only a few houses from the Sandovals. "I'm gonna go get Ernie and his dad," Abel said. "They'll get Sarah home safely."

Abel jogged down to the Sandoval house while Claudia waited with Sarah. When Ernesto came to the door, Abel explained what was happening. Ernesto's mother, Maria Sandoval, came up behind her son. "Luis is at a late history department meeting. He won't be home until around ten, but I can drive Sarah home, Abel."

"Thanks, Mrs. Sandoval," Abel said gratefully.

Maria Sandoval told Abel to stay with Ernesto in the driveway. She slipped on a sweater against the cool evening and drove to where Claudia and Sarah were standing. As she pulled up beside them. She got out of the car and told Claudia. "You can go home now. I'll take Sarah home." Claudia's house was just a few doors down from the Sandovals.

"Thanks Mrs. Sandoval," Claudia said. "This is real nice of you. Sarah and her mom's condo is at 512 Cardinal Street."

"Hello Sarah," Mrs. Sandoval said. "Get in," she offered, opening the door for her on the passenger side. "I'll have you home in a couple of minutes."

Sarah stood on the sidewalk next to the car. "You don't need to be doing this," Sarah insisted. "I often hang out at the twenty-four-seven store till ten or even later. And I walk home. My boyfriend walks with me. Mom doesn't care."

"Just get in, Sarah," Ernesto's mother ordered. "I'm sure your mom doesn't want you on the street at night. Bad things can happen."

Sarah Suarez got into the Sandovals' minivan and pulled the door shut.

"Buckle up, Sarah," Mrs. Sandoval said, as she walked around the front of the car. She checked for traffic, then opened the car door and got in.

Once inside the car, Mrs. Sandoval continued, "We always buckle up, even if we're just going a few blocks." The car pulled away from the curb.

"You got a daughter, Mrs. Sandoval?" Sarah asked.

"Yes, I have two daughters. Katalina is eight, and Juanita is six. You probably know that Abel is my son Ernie's best friend. Abel told us that you go to middle school with Abel's sister, Penny. Are you guys friends?"

"No," Sarah replied. "She's stuck-up. Most of the girls at middle school are snotty.

I got a nice boyfriend, though. And maybe him and me'll run away together. I hate my life so much. I need to get away from here."

Maria Sandoval frowned. "Honey," she said, "you're just thirteen. Thirteen-year-old girls don't run away with their boyfriends. You shouldn't even have a serious boyfriend at your age. My goodness."

"Abel Ruiz is pretty nice," Sarah went on, ignoring Mrs. Sandoval. "But that creepy four-eyes who works with him at the donut shop has her claws in him. I told Abel he was cute, but he wouldn't be friends with me. It's because of that wicked witch of the west, that Claudia Villa. But I'm much prettier than she is."

"Abel is sixteen years old, Sarah," Mrs. Sandoval remarked. "You're just a little kid to him. He's way too old for you."

Maria Sandoval pulled up in front of the condo at 512 Cardinal, and Sarah started to get out. "You can go now, Mrs. Sandoval," she suggested. "I got a key to get in. I'll just let myself in. Thanks for the ride."

"I think I'll just walk in for a minute and say 'Hi' to your mom," Mrs. Sandoval said.

"She'll be sleeping," Sarah objected.

Mrs. Sandoval got out of the car and walked to the door with Sarah. As they both went in, Maria called out softly, "Mrs. Suarez? . . . Sarah's home." There was no answer. Mrs. Sandoval shrugged, said goodnight to Sarah, and drove home.

She was in her own driveway when she noticed her purse on the floor, the wallet was on the floor beside it. Maria Sandoval was startled.

CHAPTER EIGHT

Ernesto's mother checked her wallet. It had been in her purse, which was between her and Sarah as they drove to Cardinal Street. Sometime during the short drive, the wallet left her purse, and wallet and purse wound up on the floor.

"Oh no!" Maria Sandoval cried. "I had twenty dollars in my wallet and, now it's gone."

Abel was still there, standing in the driveway with Ernesto. Abel stared at Ernesto. "Ernie, you hear what your mom's saying? That kid ripped off twenty from her purse!"

"Oh my!" Ernesto's mother moaned. "I hate to think that, but the purse was on the seat between me and Sarah. And the twenty was in there. I hate to lose twenty dollars, but I didn't actually see her take it. I don't want to get the girl in any trouble. She seems to be in a bad enough place in her life as it is."

"Abel," Ernesto recalled, "you told me and Dad how Elena Suarez is always missing money at the donut shop, and she's accusing the kids who work there. I bet this little twit has been ripping off her mom all along. I bet that's how all the money has been mysteriously disappearing."

"Yeah," Abel agreed. "I bet you're right. She gets in her mom's purse before Elena even comes to work. Then her mom is thinking the employees at the donut place are stealing from her. I bet the kid sneaked money from the cash register too. And we know she stole that tray of donuts and apple fritters. And Elena was all but accusing the poor new guy, Zeno, of taking them."

"Well," Mrs. Sandoval remarked, "there's nothing we can do about it tonight.

Of course, Elena Suarez has to be told eventually that the girl has a serious problem. If she's stealing from her mother, she's probably stealing from other people too."

Abel went home, relieved that the mystery of the vanishing money had been solved, but not sure what was coming next. He was hoping somebody else would tell Elena Suarez about Sarah's thieving. He didn't want to be the one to carry the bad news.

Abel did some math homework; then he went to bed. He was in a deep sleep when his cell phone rang. He stared at the time: two in the morning. Abel knew some wacky kids at Chavez High, but nobody would be calling him at this hour.

"Yeah?" Abel mumbled into the phone when he finally found it amid the math homework papers on his bedside table.

"Abel, this is Sarah," the girl spoke in a high-pitched, stressed-out voice. "I need your help bad, Abel. I need to get to my friend's house downtown, and somebody has got to drive me. Could you borrow your parent's car and take me downtown? This is an emergency, Abel. My mom is freaking out, and I gotta get out of here."

"How'd you get my cell phone number?" Abel asked. He never would have been fool enough to give it to her.

"Penelope gave it to me," Sarah said. "Oh please, will you help me, Abel? I'm just totally desperate."

"Sarah, listen to me," Abel commanded. "Are you nuts? I'm gonna get out of bed at two in the morning to help a thirteen-year-old kid to run away from home? I don't hardly know you, Sarah. Go back to bed, and settle the stuff with your mom in the morning."

"Please Abel!" Sarah cried. "I *know* you like me. I saw the way you were looking at me. I'd just be so grateful if you helped me. It's so horrible here with my mother, and my friend will take me in."

"It'd be a crime if I helped a kid run away from home, Sarah," Abel groaned. "I'd go to jail. You must think I'm totally crazy or something."

"My mom is gonna kill me, and then you'll be sorry," Sarah threatened.

"If it's that bad, call 911," Abel advised. "They'll come and help you and find a place for you to stay."

The phone shut disconnected at Sarah's end. Abel put his cell phone back on the table and tried unsuccessfully to go back to sleep. He didn't believe Sarah was in any danger. Elena Suarez was a maddening crazy lady, but she loved her daughter. She wouldn't harm her daughter.

At four in the morning, Liza Ruiz flung open Abel's bedroom door and cried in a hysterical voice, "Abel! Something awful has happened!"

Abel sat up so fast he almost tumbled out of bed. The first thing he could think of was that Dad had had a heart attack. He was working so hard, and he didn't look too good lately. "Mom! Is Dad okay?" Abel cried.

Mom ignored the question about Sal Ruiz. "Elena Suarez just called," she gasped.

"She said her daughter has run away from home, and she thinks you helped her. She said she caught Sarah talking to you at two in the morning. She and Sarah had a fight. Then, when she checked her room just now, the girl was gone!" Abel's mother was clutching at her head in a distraught fashion. "Oh Abel, *what have you done?*"

"I didn't do anything," Abel insisted. "The kid's a loose cannon. She's running the streets all the time. She called me last night. She wanted me to drive her to some friend's house 'cause she said her mom was beating on her. I told her to go back to bed and leave me alone."

"Abel," Mom demanded, her voice still high-pitched. "This is a thirteen-year-old *child*. Why would she call you? Have you been hanging out with her, Abel? Oh, Abel, I cannot believe this is happening. You must have given her reason to believe you'd help her. I was always worried about you. You use such bad judgment! You've made a mess of so many things—and *now this*! Abel, tell me the truth. What is between you and this *child*?"

Abel got out of bed. "Mom," Abel explained, "I work for her mother at the donut shop. Sarah came in sometimes. She flirted with me. She flirts with all the guys from Chavez. She even flirts with the gangbangers. I've seen her on the street at night. I always told her to go home. I told her she was a little girl and I was a sixteen-year-old guy. I told her to get lost. Sarah is a liar and a thief—"

"Oh Abel! Abel!" Mom groaned. "You'll be the death of me yet! Everything your brother is involved in is wonderful. You get a lousy job in a donut store, and it turns into a disaster! It's almost like you're jinxed, Abel!"

Dad and Penelope were crammed into the hallway outside Abel's room, awakened by Mom's yelling. "What's going on, Liza? What's all the hollering about?" Dad asked.

"Mrs. Suarez, Abel's boss at the donut shop, she just called," Mrs. Ruiz answered, now nearly hyperventilating. "Her thirteen-year-old daughter has run away, and she thinks our son is involved!"

"*What*?" Dad gasped. "That's nuts. That's crazy. Some little thirteen-year-old and *our son*?"

"It happens a lot," Mom declared grimly. "A lot of these thirteen-, fourteen-year-old kids hang with older boys."

Penelope piped up. "Sarah told me she was in love with Abel, but he's mean to her because he likes some older girl."

Abel's parents turned sharply and looked at Penelope. Penelope continued, "Yeah, she told me she wanted to run away with Abel, but I told her she was *loca*. Everybody at school thinks she's crazy. I think she wants to be as bad as she can be to punish her mom for splitting up with Sarah's dad."

"Oh Abel! Abel!" Mom wailed. "Why do you get mixed up in these situations?"

Anger surged in Abel's heart. "Mom, it's not my fault. You were the one who suggested I look for work at the donut shop. I didn't know the lady there was crazy. Elena Suarez is always missing money, and she blames us—the kids who work there. Turns out Sarah has been stealing from her."

"Abel," Mom asked, "why didn't you tell your father and I what was going on down there? We didn't know any of this, about the stealing, about Sarah pestering you. This is all news to us. Why didn't you let us know what was going on so it wouldn't hit us like a bombshell?"

"You know why?" Abel almost screamed. "You know why I don't tell you anything, Mom? It's 'cause of the stuff going on right now. You think I'm to blame for everything. You think I'm a stupid idiot who can't do anything right. And Tomás is a wonderful genius who can do no wrong. So I don't share stuff with you, and I never will. If I was dying of some terrible disease, I wouldn't even tell you guys anything, and you know why? You know what you'd be doing, Mom? You'd be yelling at me that I brought the disease on myself!"

Mom looked stricken. She clasped her hands to her cheeks," Oh Abel!"

The sound of crackling gravel in the driveway had distracted Penelope, who'd scurried to the hallway window.

"Mom! Dad!" Penelope yelled, "there's a cop car in the driveway!"

"Oh no! *Dios mío*!" Liza Ruiz screamed. "They've come to arrest you, Abel. *Mi hijo*!" She looked as though she was about to faint.

Sal Ruiz, who rarely intervened in anything, finally took charge. "Liza," he ordered her in a firm voice, "sit down and put a cool cloth on your head. Penelope, get a cool cloth for your mother. Just be calm, Liza. It's going to be all right."

The doorbell rang, and two officers stood on the doorstep in the early dawn darkness. The older of the pair was a woman, Sergeant Arriola. She looked about thirty-five. The younger was Officer Monez, who looked in his twenties.

"Good morning," Sergeant Arriola said. "Is Abel Ruiz at home?"

"Yes," Dad replied. "Come in. He's our son. He's right here."

The two police officers glanced at the weeping woman lying on the sofa and Penelope coming out of the kitchen with a damp cloth. Then they turned to Mr. Ruiz.

"Sir," they began on a script they probably knew well, "we'd like to speak with your son, Abel. Do we have your permission?"

"We're always willing to cooperate with the police," Mr. Ruiz replied. At that moment, Abel appeared. He had thrown a robe over his pajamas and was barefoot. His father explained that the police wanted to speak with him. Was that all right? Abel listened intently and nodded yes.

"Abel," Sergeant Arriola asked, "do you know Sarah Suarez?"

"Yeah, she's the daughter of the lady I work for at the donut shop," Abel answered.

"Did you see Sarah last night, Abel?" the sergeant asked in an unemotional voice.

"Yeah," Abel explained. "I got off work at the donut shop, and me and Claudia Villa got a yogurt. We were walking home when we ran into Sarah. It was about seven-thirty. Sarah said she was meeting her boyfriend or something. Me and Claudia told her to go home 'cause it was dangerous for a little girl like her to be on the street at night. She didn't want to go home. We called her mom. She was kinda buzzed. She wouldn't believe Sarah was out there on the street. She told us Sarah was in her bed at home."

Liza Ruiz was staring at her son as he talked. She couldn't believe how calmly he was handling this dire situation. The two officers listened intently, their eyes barely leaving Abel.

"Anyway," Abel went on, "me and Claudia didn't know what to do. 'Cause we didn't want to leave Sarah out there by herself. So we went to my friend's house . . . my friend is Ernesto Sandoval. His mom offered to drive Sarah home. And she did."

Apparently, the officers assumed that was the end of the story because they broke their gaze at him. But their eyes snapped back on him when he continued.

"Then, around two in the morning, Sarah calls me. I was sleeping. My dumb sister, Penelope goes to middle school with Sarah, and she gave Sarah my cell phone number. Anyway, Sarah's all hysterical. She's saying her mom is beating on her or something. She wants me to drive her downtown so she can hang out with a friend or something. I told her she was nuts. I told her if she's scared of her mom, she should call 911. Then Sarah hung up, and I tried to go back to sleep. Then it gets to be four in the morning, and Sarah's mom calls here, all revved up. She says Sarah ran away. Maybe I had something to do with it. But I didn't. That's all I know."

Sergeant Arriola took down the names, addresses, and phone numbers of the Sandovals and Claudia Villa.

Liza Ruiz spoke up then. "My son, Abel, he's had nothing but trouble since he started working at that donut shop. The one that Sarah's mother owns. The mother, Elena, she's been missing money all the time. Then she starts accusing my son and the other kids who work there of robbing her. But it turns out the girl, Sarah, took the money. This has been just a horrible experience for us. My son is a good boy. He's never done a bad thing in his life. It is so horrifying to have him mixed up in all this."

The sergeant nodded sympathetically. "Well, thank you for your help. I'm sure your story will check out. Here's my number in case any of you hear anything about the girl. I work the night shift. But call anytime, and I'll get back to you." The sergeant handed business cards to Mr. and Mrs. Ruiz and to Abel.

"Sarah may be anywhere," the sergeant said. "Mrs. Suarez said she has talked about going to her father. But he's apparently vanished, and nobody knows where he is. That's what Mrs. Suarez told us."

The police office looked at Abel and said, "Thank you so much. I commend you that you got your friend's mother to drive Sarah home. It's unfortunate she didn't stay there."

"Yeah," Abel agreed.

As the police officers turned to leave, Sergeant Arriola stopped to face Penelope and inquired, "So you go to school with Sarah?"

"Yeah," Penelope replied. "She's in a couple of my classes. She's really weird. She used to be okay before her parents got divorced. She kinda freaked out then. Oh, and she smokes dope too. She offered me and my friends some weed, but we wouldn't try it."

From the sofa, Lisa Ruiz wailed, "Dope! *Dios mío*! Can it get any worse?"

Sergeant Arriola glanced toward the sofa, then smiled at Penelope. "Good for you! If you remember anything that Sarah might have said, you let us know."

When the two police officers walked back to their car, the sun was coming up as a brilliant red disk in the sky.

"Thank God they didn't arrest you!" Mom declared with a shudder that seemed to rock her entire body.

"Arrest me for *what*, for cryin' out loud," Abel snapped. "Mom, excuse me for saying it. But sometimes you're a big pain, you know?"

Dad suddenly announced he had to get ready for work. And Penelope took off for her room.

A few minutes later, Abel texted Ernesto. He told him the police would probably be checking with his mother about Sarah's disappearance. Ernesto called back immediately. "What's that about the kid disappearing?"

"Yeah," Abel explained. "She ran away from home in the middle of the night. Your mom was nice enough to get her home, and then the kid split."

"Oh brother!" Ernesto groaned.

"Yeah," Abel continued. "And Elena Suarez called the cops and said maybe I knew something about her kid splitting.

Then when the cop car pulled into our driveway, good old Mom practically has a cow! Mom was sure I screwed up somehow and the cops were gonna take me away in handcuffs!"

"Oh man!" Ernesto sympathized. "You okay, dude?"

"Yeah," Abel assured his friend. "Nothin' like being rousted out of bed by a screaming mother and two cops to get a guy revved up for the day."

Ernesto laughed. Somehow that made Abel feel better. Ernesto could always make him feel better.

As the Ruiz family ate breakfast, Penelope announced, "Sarah, she was always talking about her boyfriends. But me and my friend never saw any. We never saw her with a guy. She said guys picked her up at the twenty-four-seven store and took her to the movies—high school guys. But we'd see her hanging out there, and she was always alone. She'd come on to guys, but they'd just laugh at her."

Penelope reached for the sugar for her cereal, but her hand retreated because of a laser look from Mom. She munched and talked on. "I mean, get real. She's only thirteen years old. Even the boys in middle school didn't want to be friends with her, 'cause she acts older than the rest of us. I mean, there's a boy in my math class I sorta like, and he likes me, I think. But it's no big deal. Like Miguel will bring an extra peach in his lunch for me and stuff like that. But no boy wants to do that for Sarah 'cause she's so weird."

"What a harrowing morning," Liza Ruiz declared, only dimly aware of her daughter's account of Sarah. She drank her black coffee, nibbled on a piece of toast, and groaned. "I have a headache and an upset stomach. I'm done for the day. Those scarves I've been working on can just sit there. That Suarez woman was actually screaming at me over the phone, demanding to know where Abel had gone with her little girl! Abel, don't *ever* go back to that donut shop!"

Abel concentrated on his microwaved ham and egg burrito, deep in thought. "The worst part of the whole mess," he was saying to himself, "is that Mom's first reaction is that I did something wrong or at least incredibly stupid." Mom had been that way all his life. Once, when Abel was in third grade, someone called from the school office. The caller told Mrs. Ruiz that Abel had struck another boy in the eye with a rock and that the child was rushed to the emergency room. Mom believed it immediately, even though Abel was a gentle child who never as much as pushed another student. In fact, Abel was often bullied at school because he was smaller than most kids. But he took it without retaliating.

But Mom had stormed down to the school. She headed directly for the principal's office, where Abel was supposedly being held until a parent got there.

"Where is he? Where's my son?" Mom had demanded. "I've told him over and over to never get into fights. How could this have happened? What got into the boy?"

"Oh, I'm terribly sorry, Mrs. Ruiz," the principal told her. "But there's been an awful mistake. The lady in the office who called you mixed up your son's name with the child who actually threw the rock. She called the wrong parent. *I am so sorry*. The moment I heard that Abel Ruiz was accused of the rock throwing, I *knew* it was a mistake. We've called the home of the boy who did throw the rock. But we were too late to catch you before you started down here. Believe me, Mrs. Ruiz, I know that *Abel would never do such a thing*!"

"Even in third grade," Abel thought, as he took a bite of burrito, "the principal of the elementary school knew me better than my own mother did. The principal knew I couldn't do anything like that to another kid. But Mom bought the terrible accusation at once—hook, line, and sinker." There was nothing Abel could do that was too off the wall for Mom to disbelieve.

Now Abel got up from the breakfast table. "I'm going to school now," he announced.

"Hey, *muchacho*!" Dad hailed him. "You handled yourself real well with that lady cop. I was proud of you, Abel. You were real cool."

"Thanks Dad," Abel replied. Then Abel looked at his mother.

"Abel," Mom murmured in an uneven voice. "I'm sorry if I overreacted some-what. I know you're a good, sensible boy. You wouldn't have had anything to do with that poor girl disappearing."

"Do you really know that, Mom?" Abel asked, his voice cold. "You coulda fooled me. I mean, it sounded to me like I was tried, found guilty, and sentenced right here in my own house. At four o'clock in the morning! All that was left for the cops to do was take me away." Abel couldn't remember ever using such a tone of voice to his mother before. He turned and walked out the door, slamming it behind him.

CHAPTER NINE

Abel felt bad as he walked to school. Obviously he'd lost his job at the donut shop. The money he was making had meant a lot to him. If Sarah Suarez stayed missing, her mother would be so distraught she'd probably close the place anyway. It would go the way of the hardware store and the chicken place. It'd be just another empty building with the dreaded sign in the window: "*En renta*" . . . "For lease." Only nobody ever leased them.

Poor Claudia, Abel thought. She was out of a job too. She might have to quit that private school she loved so much. It was a total bummer for all involved.

As Abel walked to school, he called Claudia. He told her everything that had happened this morning. When he was done, Claudia groaned. "Oh Abel, what a horrible thing to have happen! And to think we did the responsible thing last night and got Sarah safely home."

"Yeah," Abel went on, "and Sarah's mom, she calls my mom this morning and accuses me of helping Sarah run away. And Mom believes it! I think if the local bank was robbed, and some homeless guy said he saw me running out with a bag of money, Mom would believe him. In fact, she'd go hysterical. She'd wring her hands and babble, '*Mi hijo, mi hijo*! How could you?'"

"I'm sorry Abel. That must be rough," Claudia sympathized.

"I think the donut place will be shut down too," Abel added. "Which means we're out of jobs. Claudia, I won't miss that crazy lady, but I'll sure miss workin' with you. And I'll miss that paycheck too. You know what, Claudia, seeing you was always the highlight of my day."

"Abel, after school, come on over to my house," Claudia suggested. "Mom made some wonderful butterscotch cookies. We can sit in the swing and talk. We have a nice swing in the backyard. An old-fashioned swing with room for two. It's pretty cool."

Abel's spirits went up. "Yeah? Hey, that'd be good. I'd like that." Then he had misgivings. "You sure, Claudia?"

"Yeah, I'm sure," she replied. Her tone said "why not?" "Mom gets me home around three-thirty. So anytime after that. And hey, I'm real sorry about all you've been through. I guess Paul Morales had it right when he said working at the donut shop would hurt us all in the end."

"Yeah," Abel agreed. But for the first time since Mom yanked him out of bed with the hysterical bulletin about Sarah, Abel felt like a human being again. Looking forward to seeing Claudia in the afternoon made all the difference in his day.

And she seemed to like him too. "She must," he thought. "Or she wouldn't be asking me over to sit on her swing with her and eat her mom's butterscotch cookies."

At lunchtime at Cesar Chavez High School, Abel and his friends talked about what had happened.

"I wonder where the kid is," Ernesto asked. "I mean, it's real dangerous for a thirteen-year-old to be on the loose."

"Yeah!" responded Julio Avila, one of Ernesto's track teammates. "Just last year a fourteen-year-old girl was walking to school, and she just vanished. They never found her. Witnesses said a guy in a green pickup seemed to slow down alongside her where she was walking on the sidewalk. When they looked again, she was gone, and so was the truck."

Carlos Negrete, the former tagger, spoke. "I remember that. They had this vigil for the girl, flowers and candles. But nothing turned up. Everybody praying and crying." He shook his head.

"You think Sarah would just get in a car with a stranger?" Ernesto asked Abel.

"Yeah," Abel nodded yes. "This kid, she's nuts. I think if Frankenstein's monster would offer her a ride, she'd go with him. She'd jump right in."

Julio shook his head sadly. "Hate to see a girl heading for trouble like that. She's just a kid."

Right after lunch, Abel walked to his American history class with Luis Sandoval. It was Abel's favorite class. Abel wasn't too crazy about any class. But Mr. Sandoval made the subject interesting, and he was such a nice man that listening to him was fun. Abel couldn't wait to be done with high school and to be taking classes in some culinary school, getting ready for a career he would really enjoy.

After history class, Mr. Sandoval nodded toward Abel. "See you for a minute?"

"Sure," Abel said and stood by the teacher's desk until the other students cleared out.

"Abel," Mr. Sandoval confided, "the police came over this morning to talk to us about my wife driving Sarah home last night. Maria wanted to talk to Sarah's mother, but she couldn't rouse her. Sarah said she was sleeping. It's a real sad situation. I was gladder than ever you'd talked to Ernie and me about the problems you were having with Mrs. Suarez. That talk kind of gave me an insight. Poor Mrs. Suarez. Not holding it together too well. How about you, Abel? Are you okay?"

"Yeah, sure Mr. Sandoval," Abel assured him. "My mom freaked out when the police came to our house this morning. She was sure I was gonna be arrested for something. I mean, she thought I had to have done something stupid to have caused all this trouble. Mom thinks I'm the stupidest person who ever lived." Abel sounded bitter.

"I'm sure she doesn't think that, Abel," Ernesto's father objected. "She's just the nervous type. She's very excitable. I saw that when we had that delicious salmon dinner at your house. Your mom looked frozen in fear that somehow it wouldn't turn out well. That's sad, because you can't enjoy the occasion when you're that uptight."

"Yeah," Abel agreed. "Mom had the pizzeria number handy in case I blew it, which she expected. That way, we could get the pepperoni pizza rolling for you guys." His voice now sounded angry.

"Well Abel," Mr. Sandoval advised, "parents don't always get it right, you know. I've got two daughters—little ones—and they're so different. Katalina, she's eight, and it seems to me she's really strong. Juanita, she's six, and she's more vulnerable. I'm always wanting to protect her more. But the other night, we had that freak electrical storm, with all that thunder and lightning. I head for Juanita's room because I think she needs some hugs and reassurances. She was fine. But I don't even think about Katalina. I pass her room, and she's sitting up in bed, her eyes real wide. I can see she's scared stiff. I was really surprised. I went in there and got her big fuzzy black bear down from the shelf. Then she and I and the bear sort of snuggled until the thunder passed."

Mr. Sandoval dropped his glance down, at the desk, recalling the moment. "She looks at me with these big eyes, always so full of confidence. Then she says, 'Thank you, Daddy.' See what I mean, Abel? Don't be too hard on your mom. She loves you, Abel. When that salmon dinner turned out so well, she was just beaming. Man, she was drinking in the compliments like they were fine wine. She was proud of you, Abel."

"I guess so," Abel admitted. "But it's tough when your parents don't have faith in you. I remember when I played Little League, all the parents would be yelling to their kids, 'You can do it! Hang in there!' Then there would be Mom yelling, 'Don't worry, Abel. It's all right if you can't do it.'"

"Hang in there, Abel," Mr. Sandoval counseled. "You'll be fine. And someday your parents will laugh at themselves and say, 'Wow, we never dreamed the kid was that good, that he'd go this far!' And then, Abel, it will be all the sweeter."

Abel smiled at Luis Sandoval. He needed a pep talk, and Mr. Sandoval delivered. He always did.

As Abel walked home after school, he felt bad that he wouldn't be going to work anymore. He had started to enjoy the routine. Going to work and earning money had made him feel like a man. As he walked past Elena's Donut Shop, to his surprise, a man was inside—about forty. Curious, Abel wondered up to the door.

"Hi," Abel greeted him.

"Hi," the man said. "Want something, kid?"

"I used to work here," Abel commented forlornly. "I worked for Elena Suarez until yesterday."

"You know what happened?" the man asked.

"Yeah, Sarah, her daughter ran away," Abel replied.

"I'm Hector Ponce, Elena's brother," the man introduced himself. "My sister is pretty messed up with the kid missing. Nobody knows where she is. But Elena needs money coming in. Her ex don't send her anything. I'm gonna be runnin' the donut shop until things get back to normal. I was gonna text you guys to come back to work. We need you. Who're you?"

"Abel Ruiz," Abel answered, his heart racing.

Ponce looked at a chart he was holding. "Yeah, she likes you. You're Monday, Wednesday, and Friday, four to seven, right? I'm gonna text this Claudia Villa and Zeno Rodriguez. You okay with coming in as usual, Abel?"

"You bet!" Abel said enthusiastically. "I'm going over to Claudia's house now, and I'll give her the good news that we still got jobs."

"Cool," Ponce acknowledged. "My sister, she ain't the sharpest knife in the drawer on a good day. But now, with the kid

AWOL, she's bonkers, you know what I mean? I loaned Elena the money to start this business. So I got a stake here too. If the joint goes down the drain, I'm out a lot of money. Life goes on. Bills have to be paid. That's the way of the world."

"Has the family any idea where Sarah went?" Abel asked.

Hector Ponce stood there without much expression on his face. "Who knows? She was a loose cannon. She didn't get along with her mother. Who does get along with Elena? Anyhow, Sarah, she was a daddy's girl. When Elena sent daddy packing, the kid flipped. I think she's gone for good."

Abel turned cold. "Gone?" he repeated.

"Yeah," Hector Ponce nodded. "You know how it is. Kid that age goes missing. Some cop on TV, he says you take any street corner, and there's a predator there. You can count on a creep being there. Sarah, she was a beauty. She was the kind they look for."

Hector Ponce kept talking about Sarah in the past tense. Abel felt sick to his stomach. He didn't know Sarah well at all, but she was a young girl who had crossed his path. He didn't want her to be gone. It wasn't fair. She was only thirteen years old. She deserved a lifetime. She was a pain in the neck, and she was foolish. But she had her whole life ahead of her. She could still be set straight. It wasn't fair if something happened to her.

"Well, see you tomorrow, Abel," Hector Ponce said, ending the discussion. He didn't seem very shaken by the possibility that his niece was gone. "The beat goes on, eh?"

Abel walked on. He thought about Sarah's desperate phone call. He was half asleep when she called. He was angry that she had awakened him at two in the morning. He tried to remember now what she had said. Maybe she'd given him a clue that he could take to the police. She said she wanted to go downtown to a friend's house. Did a friend offer to take her in, or was it another lie, another of her fantasies? Abel wondered, had Sarah found someone else to take her downtown? Was she right now holed up with a friend while her mother went crazy worrying about her?

Abel called Penelope on his cell phone. He asked her whether Sarah ever mentioned having a friend downtown.

"She'd always be talking about friends who lived in different places," Penelope rattled on. "Boyfriends, girlfriends. I don't think any of them ever existed. She told me once she hung out with an exchange student from Greece. Then she laughed and said it was a joke. When her parents broke up, I guess she didn't like her world anymore. So she made up a new one filled with all kinds of fake people."

"Okay, Penny, thanks," Abel said. "If you think of anything else she might've said that'd, you know, give the cops a clue to where she went, let me know."

Abel walked along Tremayne. He turned on Wren Street. His steps quickened. He was eager to see Claudia. That was his only bright spot right now. He hoped she'd be willing to go back to work at the donut shop too. He wasn't sure he could work there now without her. Abel dreaded the thought of being out of work and pounding the pavement again, looking for another job—and probably not finding anything. He'd have to put off his dream of having a car. Even if he could get a car with the thousand dollars he already had, he needed money for gas, insurance, and other stuff.

"Hi Abel," Claudia greeted him. She'd changed out of her school uniform. She now wore jeans and a pretty T-shirt. She looked great.

"Claudia, I got news," Abel declared. "I walked by the donut shop, and Elena's brother was there getting it ready to reopen. He said his sister is too upset to run it, but she needs the income; so he's gonna run it for her. His name is Hector Ponce, and he offered me my job back. And he said to tell you you could come back too if you wanted. Whaddya think, Claudia?"

"Oh Abel, that's great!" Claudia exclaimed, her face breaking into a smile. "Wow, what a relief! Last night me and my parents were going over the family budget. It looked like, if I didn't get another job in a hurry, I'd have to quit my school and go to Chavez. I was just sick about it. I felt so bad and my parents did too. But Dad's insurance commissions are down, and we're really right on the edge with the big mortgage and everything. Abel, of course I want to go back. You're going too, right?"

"Yeah, for sure if you are," Abel responded with a grin. "My mom won't like it. But—you know what, Claudia?—I'm sick of being cowed by her. When I get home tonight, I'm telling Mom a different person is running the place and there's nothing to be afraid of. I'm sixteen years old, and I've never gotten in any trouble. It's time Mom gives me a little credit. I'm almost a man, Claudia, and it's time I start acting like one."

"Here! Here!" Claudia cried.

They went into the backyard and sat in the swing, which rocked lazily back and forth. Claudia's mother brought butterscotch cookies on paper plates, and she put down a jug of *agua fresca* and paper cups. She was a pretty woman but looked nothing like Claudia. Abel thought Claudia must resemble her father.

"These are good," Abel commented, sampling a cookie. "Not too sweet, but delicious. And the consistency is just right too."

Mrs. Villa smiled and acknowledged his compliment. "Thank you."

"Mom," Claudia said, "he's going to be a chef. Remember I told you how he cooked a salmon dinner for ten people a couple weeks ago? So when he compliments your cookies, you can feel honored!"

Mrs. Villa laughed and made a little curtsy. Abel liked her. When Abel and Claudia were alone, Abel started talking about something that was bothering him. "I was surprised how Elena's brother talked about Sarah. I mean, his niece is missing, and something could've happened to her. But he didn't seem to care. He said he didn't think she'd ever come back. Then he shrugs and goes, 'The beat goes on.' Real creepy guy."

"Boy!" Claudia remarked. "But I don't agree with him that Sarah is gone for good. She's hanging out somewhere. She just wants to make her mom suffer because she got rid of Sarah's father. You know, I bet Sarah would love to go find her father, but I guess she has no idea where he is. Elena said he intentionally vanished so he couldn't get stuck paying any support money."

"Yeah, I thought of the father too," Abel agreed. "I guess there's a lot of guys like that out there. I think they call them 'dead-beat dads' or something. I've even seen photos of them in the post office. The government wants to find them 'cause the state ends up supporting a lot of these mothers and kids."

Later, when Abel got home, his mother was in the living room, putting the finishing touches on two of her beautiful scarves.

"Hi Abel," she greeted him, still feeling guilty about this morning. "Did you have a nice day at school?"

"Yeah Mom," Abel responded. "I got good news. I thought I lost my job at the donut shop, but Elena's brother is taking over. He said I could come back and work there."

"Abel!" Mom gasped. "After all the trauma we've been through because of the people at that place, I cannot believe you are considering going back there. Abel, you cannot do it. You absolutely cannot—"

"I'm not *considering* going back there, Mom," Abel asserted. "I *am* going back there. It's all settled."

Abel stood in the middle of the room, his hands on his hips, glaring at his mother. "I want to make more money and get my car. I want to have change for stuff like going out once in a while. I like the work.

It's easy. I'm good at it, and I'm getting experience. I probably couldn't get another job anyway. It makes me feel like a man to have real work to do and not just be going back and forth to school like a little kid."

Liza Ruiz stared at her son as if she was seeing him for the first time. She *was* seeing him for the first time, in a way. He had turned into an entirely different person. He looked like Abel Ruiz—her inept, weak child who was lovable and obedient to her every whim. But he wasn't *that* Abel Ruiz anymore.

"Abel," Liza Ruiz replied in a faltering voice. "I just hope you know what you're doing, going back to that awful place and working there again."

"I do know what I'm doing," Abel stated flatly, before turning and going to his room.

CHAPTER TEN

Being back in the donut shop after school the next day, Wednesday, felt good. Abel had already learned that routine can be comforting. Many of the regular customers were complaining about the one day the shop was closed. The heavy man who always wanted three dozen assorted donuts said he didn't know what to do. Finally he went to the supermarket. "But the donuts over there aren't nearly as good as here," he noted, smiling as he peered into the display case again to make his choices.

Abel was so glad to be back at work that he wasn't even annoyed at how long the big man took to choose his three dozen donuts.

Claudia, Abel, and Zeno worked steadily, doling out glazed and chocolate donuts, bear claws, and apple fritters. Hector Ponce spent most of his time in the back room. And he pretty much kept out of the crew's way, which they all appreciated.

During a lull, Abel asked Claudia whether Elena had ever said where her husband had gone to. Didn't she have a clue?

Claudia shook her head. "Elena's the kind of person who's not much interested in the people around her, even her family. If her husband had favorite places where he talked about retiring to or something, she wouldn't have even listened. She's totally self-centered." Claudia said.

The shift went smoothly, and Abel was in a good mood until just before quitting time. Then something bad happened. Elena Suarez showed up. Her face was red and swollen as if she had been crying all day. And she probably had been. She glanced at Claudia and Abel. Then she quickly looked away and hurried to her brother in the back room. Abel overheard some of the conversation between brother and sister.

"Anything yet?" Hector asked in a disinterested voice.

"Not a word, Hector," Elena responded. "I'm telling you, I'm devastated. How could she have done this to me? I love that child with all my heart. She's my life. I know she was upset when the marriage ended, but that wasn't my fault. I'd stood that awful man as long as I could. Martin never treated me decently, but he indulged Sarah. She was his little pet. I don't think I could have stayed in the marriage as long as I did except for Sarah. I knew how much she loved her father and how much he loved her. I feel awful saying this, Hector. But sometimes I was jealous of Sarah . . . that my husband cared so much for her and so little for me. I was jealous of my own child. Yes, sometimes I was mean to her, but I always loved her. I can't believe she's doing this to me."

"Maybe she ain't got no choice, *hermana*," Hector told her.

"What are you saying, Hector?" Elena demanded shrilly.

"Maybe," Hector explained, "you know, the kid was hanging out there on the street. Maybe somebody come along, you know, and took her. Stuff like that happens."

Elena Suarez began sobbing loudly. "She's . . . she's not dead. I know she's not dead. A mother knows in her heart if something has happened to her child, and I know she's alive!" Elena wailed.

"Shhh!" Hector quieted her. "Customers out there. You're gonna scare them away. Get a hold of yourself, Elena."

Abel disliked Elena Suarez when she accused him and Paul of stealing from her. He almost hated her when she told his mother he might have had something to do with Sarah's disappearance. But now he couldn't help feeling sorry for her. Having a child missing had to be terrible.

Abel turned and looked through the doorway to the back room. He saw Elena Suarez sitting in a chair, her face in her hands. The woman's life was nothing special. Her marriage had failed. She had a business only because of her brother's help. All she had to show for her life was a beautiful child—Sarah. And now Sarah was gone. She had fought with Sarah, worried about her, failed to take care of her as well as she should have. But still she loved her. She didn't want to live anymore if she had lost her for good. Now, all the frustration Elena Suarez ever had with Sarah drifted away in the deep, dark river of her loss.

Finally Elena left. She walked out of the donut shop, looking neither right nor left, and vanished into the twilight outside. She didn't even notice the three giggling teenagers coming the other way, girls like Sarah. They looked about sixteen, or how Sarah would look in three years—*or how she would have looked*.

By the end of his shift, Abel was sorry for Elena. He forced himself to think about something else as he walked out with Claudia.

"I'm getting my car maybe next week," Abel commented.

"What kind of a car?" Claudia asked.

"Me and Ernie found a couple that're possibilities," Abel said. "We found a silver-colored Toyota Celica. But it's a 1984, way older than me! They said it works good, but it's got like two hundred thousand miles on it. I could get it for a thousand dollars."

"You need something newer, Abel," Claudia suggested.

"I saw a VW Jetta, white," Abel countered. "I really liked it. It was decent. 1994. But it costs two hundred dollars more than I got. I could wait until I earned more money, but then it'll be gone."

Paul Morales and a couple homies were coming in the opposite direction. "Hey Claudia, Abel," he hailed them. "So the joint opened up again, huh? But without her."

"Yeah," Abel answered. "You probably heard about Sarah disappearing."

"Yeah, the kid couldn't take the old *bruja* anymore. Can you blame her?" Paul remarked.

"Elena is really torn up about it," Claudia said.

"Hey, I'm cryin'!" Paul laughed. "Like I said, what goes around comes around. She treated people like dirt, and now it's coming back at her."

"What do you think happened to Sarah?" Claudia asked.

Paul looked at the two homies with him, and they smirked like they knew something. Paul explained. "Last I heard, the kid was trying to hitch a ride downtown. She was standing on a street corner or something. I didn't see it myself, you know, but that's what I heard." The three boys, including Paul, snickered.

Abel thought Paul had a strange look on his face, as though he knew more about what happened to Sarah than he was admitting.

"You think somebody picked her up, Paul?" Abel asked.

"Who knows?" Paul shrugged. "The middle of the night, a skinny little chick standing there trying to thumb a ride. Hey, somebody mighta taken pity on her and brought her where she wanted to go." Paul turned to his homes, "Ain't that right, dudes?"

"Yeah," one of them remarked. "Pretty *muchacha* like her, she could get in bad trouble on the street alone."

Claudia looked right at Paul. "Paul, do you know what happened to Sarah?" she asked.

"Claudia," Paul answered, "I like you. You're a great girl. But you're not one of us, you hear me? I'm just sayin' probably somebody give her a ride. And why not?"

"Paul," Claudia advised, "if you know something, you need to tell the police. Sarah's a thirteen-year-old child. The police are looking for her, and they're treating it as a possible crime."

186

Paul looked back at Claudia, a hard smile on his lips. "I don't know nothing, girl." Then he and his friends walked off laughing.

When Paul and the others were gone down the street, Abel asked Claudia, "Waddya think?"

Claudia frowned. "I'm scared that Paul or one of those other guys picked her up and took her downtown. Maybe they let her out where she said her friend was, but there wasn't any friend. Sarah was downtown, alone, with all those weirdos, some of them not so good."

"But why would Paul do something like that?" Abel asked. "Just to get even with Elena?"

"Know what, Abel?" Claudia disclosed. "Elena didn't stop at humiliating Paul by making him give her his wallet and turn his pockets inside out. She did something else. After he stormed out, she called the police. She told them she thought he'd stolen money from her. He warned her not to do that, but she did anyway. When the cops came around and hassled him, Paul went ballistic. They didn't have enough to arrest him, but he was furious. He texted me and told me he was going to get back at Elena one way or another."

"Oh man!" Abel groaned. "But to put a kid like Sarah in danger just to get even with Elena? I didn't think Paul was capable of that."

"Abel," Claudia insisted, "if he did give Sarah a ride, then she convinced him she'd be fine with her girlfriend downtown. Paul doesn't know how Sarah lies and makes up people she claims to know. He might've thought he was helping the girl out. She told you her mom was beating her. And she probably told him the same thing. Paul probably thought he was doing a good thing for the girl and sticking it to Elena at the same time."

"But poor Sarah!" Abel said. "She's probably wandering around downtown. I mean, anything could happen to a kid like that."

"We don't know for sure if that even happened, Abel. Maybe Paul was just lying," Claudia suggested.

"Where would a kid like that go?" Abel asked. "Who'd take her in where she'd be safe?"

"Her father," Claudia guessed. "But he's vanished, and Elena made sure Sarah couldn't even try to contact him."

As they walked, the cloudiness cleared up, and stars filled the night sky. A warm wind came up, stirring Claudia's long, dark hair. Abel looked over at her and told her, "Man, you're pretty."

"Oh, I am not!" Claudia giggled.

"Yes, you are," Abel insisted. "You give me goose bumps."

Claudia giggled some more. She reached over and slipped her hand into Abel's. Abel tightened his fingers around her soft little hand. They kept on walking like that, hand in hand. Abel had seen a lot of kids at Chavez walking like that, even freshmen. Here he was a junior, and it had never happened to him until now.

Suddenly Claudia sniffed the air. "Do you smell that sweetness? What is that?"

"Yeah, I smell it," Abel said.

Claudia tugged on Abel's hand and pointed with her other. "Look over there. Look at that big white flower. It's blooming in the dark! Usually flowers close up at night. It's magical looking."

"Is that what smells so good?" Abel asked.

They drew closer, and the aroma became almost overpowering.

"It's a night blooming cereus," Claudia declared. "I've seen them before. They bloom for just one night, and in the morning they're gone. They open up in the dark. They're so beautiful and sweet smelling."

"That's amazing," Abel commented. "How did you know that? It's kinda sad, though, that it only blooms for one night."

"Yeah, it's fragile, like life," Claudia mused. "Like love. I remember the first time I ever saw one of these flowers. I was a little girl walking with my dad. He said the night blooming cereus has a message for us. Cherish every moment of joy, be happy when you can. If you're grumpy and dissatisfied when times are good, then you can't survive when dark times come."

Abel turned and looked at Claudia. He had an urge to lean over and kiss her. She looked so lovely, so endearing. Abel reached gently for her shoulders, bent toward her, and brushed a kiss across her brow.

"Oh Abel," Claudia sighed, "that was so nice. I'll always remember we were standing by a night blooming cereus the first time you kissed me. And we were surrounded by the flower's fragrance."

A feeling of happiness came over Abel. Claudia had said "the first time you kissed me." Didn't that mean there would be other times? He thought that's what it meant. He hoped that's what it meant.

They walked on then, as if nothing special had happened. But something special *had* happened. Abel had never kissed a girl like that before. Once, when he was a freshman, he was dancing with a girl he hardly knew. She asked him to kiss her, and it didn't go well. For one thing, she was taller than Abel. He had meant to kiss her on the lips but ended up kissing her on the chin. The girl laughed and told Abel he was a terrible kisser. Abel had no feeling for the girl. So the kiss didn't mean anything more than a moment of embarrassment. But his feeling for Claudia was growing. Every day he felt closer to her.

Abel went to sleep that night wondering about Sarah Suarez. As he drifted off, he imagined her wandering around the downtown, looking for a friendly face and not finding any. Then his dream turned horrifying. Dozens of people were searching in a brushy ravine, and somebody shouted, "We found her!" Almost at once people were crying. Elena Suarez would never stop crying.

Abel awoke with a jolt. He sat up in bed. Sarah's sassy, pretty face remained vividly in his mind, even in the darkness of his room. She was standing there boldly, staring at him. "I want to live with my dad," she cried, in her strident voice. And then Abel remembered something Sarah had told him, something he'd completely forgotten until this moment.

"Me and Daddy were close, but she made his life miserable. Now he's in Rosarito Beach at Uncle Hilario's crab shack."

Maybe it was just another lie, another of Sarah's fantasies. Maybe she wanted so badly to know where her father was that she made up a story. Or maybe not. The father did very much love his daughter. Maybe he'd found a way to communicate with her. Maybe, unknown to Elena, she had been in touch with her father all along. Maybe, finally, he asked her to come live with him. Maybe Paul or one of his homies dropped her off at the bus station downtown, and she took the bus south to Mexico.

Abel hadn't thought of Sarah's words until the terrible dream had somehow jolted his memory. Now he leaned over in bed and grabbed his cell phone. He dialed the number on Sergeant Arriola's card.

When Arriola came on the line, Abel said, "Hi, this is Abel Ruiz. Something just came to me that Sarah Suarez said quite a while ago. I wasn't paying much attention when she said it. And like she lies a lot. So I figured it was just a fantasy or something, and maybe it is. But she said she knew her father was in Rosarito Beach with Uncle Hilario at a crab shop. She said she'd like to go there. Anyway, the minute I remembered it, I wanted to let you guys know."

"Thank you, Abel," Sergeant Arriola replied. She verified the information and then told him, "We'll contact the Mexican police and check it out right away."

Abel sank back on the pillow, his eyes wide open.

The Mexican police located Sarah Suarez with her father the next day. What Abel suspected was true. Paul or a friend had driven her to the bus station. She'd gone directly to her father and had been there ever since.

When Abel went to work at the donut shop, Hector told him that his sister had gone immediately down to Rosarito Beach to be reunited with her daughter.

"Elena, she's learned a lot in all this," Hector told Abel. "She knew the kid was aching for her father, and she just ignored that. She should have made arrangements, you know, so Sarah could visit with the Dad. All that's gonna be different now. Elena, she's gonna try to work things out so they can share custody of the girl."

A week later, Elena Suarez appeared at the donut shop. She was very calm. Abel overheard her talking to her brother. "Sarah is staying in Rosarito Beach for another week. Then she's agreed to come home with me. But she can always visit her father when she wants to. I promised her that. Martin and I even had a civilized conversation for the first time in a long time. When I was ready to leave, Sarah really touched my heart. She told me she was sorry she had hurt me so much. We had a good, long hug."

Elena then came out to the counter where Abel was working then. "Abel, I know I hurt you and humiliated you when I made you and Paul empty your wallets and your pockets. I'm very sorry for that. Sergeant Arriola told me you gave her the tip that helped them find Sarah. I had no idea her father was there. Sarah must have secretly gotten in touch with him. If you hadn't remembered what she'd said, I'd still be living in torment. Thank you, Abel." She then handed Abel an envelope, smiled at Claudia, and left.

Inside the envelope was a note that said, "Abel, there are no words to thank you for what you did. You gave me back my daughter. Here's a token of my gratitude."

Paper-clipped to the note were two hundred-dollar bills.

The amount was exactly what Abel needed to buy the VW Jetta. And he bought it the following Saturday.

The first passenger in the car was Claudia Villa.

"You know, Claudia," Abel said, as he opened the car door for her. "I feel like I learned a big lesson the last week or so." Abel got behind the wheel. He put the key in the ignition but didn't start the engine.

"I'm not sure what you mean, Abel," the girl responded.

"Well," Abel explained, "you go to school. And the teachers teach you all this stuff. Math. History. You know. And you gotta study and make the best grades you can, of course. But the teachers can't teach you some things."

Abel was struggling to express himself. He wasn't used to talking about what he thought and felt. "You know," he went on, "they can't teach you how to have a dream."

Claudia, touched, just listened. Abel continued.

"Ernesto, *mi amigo*, he said I oughta try to be a cook. That never dawned on me. But it was something I'd been thinkin' about for a long time. I just never knew it. So then I wanted to make dinner for everybody. But, as usual, Mom stood there, right in the way. I didn't want to hurt her. I love her. But she stood between me and what I needed to do. You see what I'm saying, Claudia?"

Claudia nodded yes.

"I had a dream all along," Abel mused. "Now, all I have to do is catch it."

Abel looked over at this beautiful girl who listened so attentively. He kissed her on the lips. And she kissed him back.